THE WIFE OF HIS YOUTH

"THIS IS THE WOMAN, AND I AM THE MAN" (page 24)

THE WIFE
OF
HIS YOUTH

AND OTHER STORIES OF
THE COLOR LINE

———

CHARLES W. CHESNUTT

With illustrations by Clyde O. De Land

Ann Arbor Paperbacks
THE UNIVERSITY OF MICHIGAN PRESS

First edition as an Ann Arbor Paperback 1968
All rights reserved
Published in the United States of America by
The University of Michigan Press and simultaneously
in Rexdale, Canada, by Ambassador Books Limited
Originally published in Boston in 1899
United Kingdom agent: The Cresset Press

Manufactured in the United States of America

INTRODUCTION

by Earl Schenck Miers

Charles Waddell Chesnutt was born in Cleveland, Ohio, seven years before the War Between the States ended. His parents, both natives of North Carolina, were, as it has become polite to say, "of Negro extraction." The lad's father, Andrew J., served four years in the war while young Charles was beginning his education in Cleveland; but to the elder Chesnutts, a love for the reddish hills and "lonesome pines" of North Carolina eventually proved irresistible and so the family "went home."

For the first American Negro literary figure of enduring distinction, the intellectual wrench must have been great. That Charles survived the ordeal may well demonstrate the truth in Carolyn Shipman's sentimental comment on how "talent develops itself in spite of mediocre teachers." Writing in *The Critic,* Miss Shipman was quite carried away

by the fact that by the age of sixteen Charles
had become, in the parlance of Reconstruction, a "pupil-teacher," although if he had
known no more than his multiplication tables
to the rule of ten, he could have qualified for
this distinction. In after-school hours, however, as Miss Shipman loyally noted, he
gained "by private study and wide reading"
a knowledge of the classics, French, German,
and "of pure English and of general literature." At this point Miss Shipman nearly
lost her head over Charles: "Like many literary men of the present generation (1899),
he received his college training from life. He
was his own professor . . . ."

Actually, Charles deserved all the praise
Miss Shipman heaped upon him, and perhaps
a little more. His first story, according to
The National Cyclopaedia, was written when
he was fourteen and was published in a North
Carolina newspaper. Other sources dispute
this claim. But on one point everyone agrees:
Charles was an alert, intelligent, ambitious
young man, with a keen inner ear for remem-
bering the dialect around him and with an
enormous sensitivity enabling him to understand what the tragedy of slavery had been

and what the heartbreak of Reconstruction would become.

Even his appointment as principal of the State Normal School at Fayetteville at the age of twenty-three could not hold Charles in the South for more than another two years; thereafter, as he would have heard one of his North Carolina friends tell it, he headed "Norf" until he reached New York City. Here he found employment as a reporter for a Wall Street news agency and as a contributor of a financial gossip column to the *Mail and Express*. After six months he wearied of these chores, and his path, like his heart and memory, turned toward Cleveland, where he had begun life. The New York, Chicago, and St. Louis Railroad Company hired him as a stenographer, and at the same time he studied law in the office of Judge Samuel E. Williamson, who later became counsel for the New York Central Railroad.

After many years, because of the sound training with Judge Williamson, Charles ultimately rose to the front rank of Cleveland's legal profession. In 1878 his happy marriage to Susan Perry began. Two of their daughters graduated from Smith College, and a son attended Harvard.

Just when the old literary urge once more took hold of Charles is difficult to say. Miss Shipman gives 1885 as the date of his first professional work—"a pathetic tale of Southern life" entitled "Uncle Peter's House." Perhaps earlier tales had come from Chesnutt's pen; a great many followed during the next twenty years—years when, in a manner almost incomprehensible today, the American Negro was undergoing enormous sociological and cultural changes.

Of course, Charles Waddell Chesnutt was only one of the dynamic personalities who produced a social revolution in "Black America" at the close of the nineteenth century. In such books as *Emancipation: Its Course and Progress from 1481 B.C. to A.D. 1875,* published in 1882, and *The Black Phalanx,* the story of the Negro in the Civil War, which appeared in 1888, the colored man was seen groping for the fuller life that had been promised but not yet granted. The Negro recognized that among his severest handicaps was a lack of self-esteem, and leaders arose who intended to awaken in their people a respect for their past and a belief in their future. In *Harriet, the Moses of Her People* (1886), Sarah Bradford dramatized the life of Harriet Tubman; and thirteen years later Chesnutt himself wrote the biography of Frederick Douglass. Before these had come the monumental labor of the Pennsylvanian George Washington Williams, who was to be called the "Negro Bancroft" when in 1883 G. P. Putnam's Sons published in two volumes his painstakingly thorough *History of the Negro Race in America from 1619 to 1880.*

Clearly, in the years when Chesnutt's intellect was ripening, "Black America" was in ferment. Its leaders varied from the docile Booker T. Washington (whose splendid *Story of the Negro* appeared in 1909) to the more militant W. E. B. DuBois, whose *The Suppression of the African Slave Trade, 1638–1870,* the first publication in the Harvard Historical Studies, was properly hailed as "a landmark in the intellectual growth of the American Negro."[1] Negro-oriented books and

---

[1] John Hope Franklin, *From Slavery to Freedom* (New York, 1947), p. 403.

meetings devoted to soul-searching seemed to spring up like insects in summer. The titles and subjects of these studies and conferences revealed graphically the sweeping extent of this ferment: "Some Efforts of Negroes for Social Betterment," "The Negro in Business," "The College-bred Negro," and "The Negro Common School."[2]

If Chesnutt's creative mind grew aflame in so heated a climate of intellectual awakening, one can little wonder. Aside from William Wells Brown, whose last book, *My Southern Home,* appeared in 1880, Chesnutt was the first American Negro writer of significance, and it is possible that Brown would have been impertinent to compare himself to Chesnutt. His stories, either syndicated by newspapers or appearing in such periodicals as *Puck, Tid-Bits, Two Tales, The Independent, The Overland Monthly,* and *The Atlantic Monthly,* revealed so much rich vitality, passion, wit, insight, and pathos that no one greatly marveled when other critics echoed Miss Shipman's enthusiasm. Indeed, she recorded what the critics wrote "from Maine

[2] *Ibid.,* p. 401.

to California"; some called him better than
"a cousin once removed" but a brother to
Uncle Remus, describing Chesnutt as "a new
character in whose portraits 'there is not a
line out of place.' "

Both the critics and Miss Shipman were
correct—Charles Chesnutt deserved his ac-
colade as a spinner of "fresh, vivid, dramatic
sketches" in "a new and delightful vein."
Actually, they were more than that—they
were literature.

The old century was in its last year when
three books by Chesnutt appeared: his biography of Douglass, *The Conjure Woman*
(described by *The Oxford Campanion to
American Literature* as "a series of dialect
stories about incidents of slavery, told by
an old Negro gardener to his Northern em-
ployers"), and *The Wife of His Youth*, a
collection of stories. There were to be other
novels, none of which added to his reputation: in 1900 *The House Behind the Cedars*,
in 1901 *The Marrow of Tradition*, and, four
years later, *The Colonel's Dream*.

The themes of these later and lesser works
reveal his tortured soul. In the first a Negress

wrestles with her conscience: shall she be a white man's mistress or the faithful lover of a man of her own race? The second recounts "the struggles of Negro and white half-sisters"; and the third bemoans the failure of an idealist to free a Southern town of race hatred. One almost feels Chesnutt tearing at his own flesh and heart as he deals with these complexities of the race problem; but somehow his talent never fell easily into the pattern of the novel.

With his shorter sketches—those gems of literary craftsmanship that fill the pages of *The Conjure Woman* and *The Wife of His Youth*—Chesnutt may well rank with such American masters of the craft as Mark Twain and Bret Harte, with both of whom he shared an intensity of feeling for the rawness of an emergent America. Today's advocates of "black power" may find it difficult to discover an affinity of emotional depth between Chesnutt and themselves, but that is their tragedy and not his.

For the genius of Charles Waddell Chesnutt belonged to his age as intrinsically as claws belong to a lobster. He spoke open-heartedly. He dealt with torment and hell—sometimes

with pathos and sober passion, but more
often with a sly wit and even a sense of
hilarity that was like an ax cutting into a
tree in the backwoods of the North Carolina
he knew so well. If you wish to test this truth
in the pages of the present colllection, I suggest that you read Chesnutt's dignified opening tale with its heartrending conflict of a
free Negro's loyalty to the wife he had married while a slave and to the more refined
"blue vein" Negress he meets later, and then
turn to "The Passing of Grandison," where
with high humor Chesnutt preserves forever
what the cause, course, and aftermath of the
"wah" meant to the degradation of the South.

Sometimes, with a force rarely equaled,
Chesnutt drives home these themes so well
that they can never be forgotten. The shal-
lowness—the indecency—of so-called Southern justice (in Philadelphia, Mississippi, or
elsewhere) has never been more dramatically
portrayed than in the fate that befalls Ben
Davis in "The Web of Circumstance"; in a
single sentence, "For stoicism is a savage
virtue," Chesnutt captures an elemental
truth that the present generation might well
contemplate. And who requires a more tell-

ing indictment of a sick civilization than the single sign in "The Bouquet":

"Notice. This cemetery is for white people only. Others please keep out."

Read "The Sheriff's Children" and ever try again to believe that Southern culture rose to the level of compassion required to compensate those poor black devils it had subjugated in spirit after bringing them to America in chains.

Why Charles Waddell Chesnutt gave up writing in 1905 is hard to say. Perhaps he had said all that was in his heart. Perhaps he sensed that the ameliorating influence of a Booker T. Washington was being swept aside by a more militant faction of which he never could be a genuine compatriot. A highly respected citizen and lawyer, he lived quietly with his family until his death in Cleveland on November 15, 1932.

Edison, New Jersey

CONTENTS

LIST OF ILLUSTRATIONS

THE WIFE OF HIS YOUTH

I

MR. RYDER was going to give a ball.
There were several reasons why this was an
opportune time for such an event.

Mr. Ryder might aptly be called the dean
of the Blue Veins. The original Blue Veins
were a little society of colored persons organized in a certain Northern city shortly after
the war. Its purpose was to establish and
maintain correct social standards among a
people whose social condition presented almost
unlimited room for improvement. By accident, combined perhaps with some natural
affinity, the society consisted of individuals
who were, generally speaking, more white than
black. Some envious outsider made the suggestion that no one was eligible for membership who was not white enough to show blue
veins. The suggestion was readily adopted
by those who were not of the favored few,

and since that time the society, though possessing a longer and more pretentious name, had been known far and wide as the " Blue Vein Society," and its members as the " Blue Veins."

The Blue Veins did not allow that any such requirement existed for admission to their circle, but, on the contrary, declared that character and culture were the only things considered ; and that if most of their members were light-colored, it was because such persons, as a rule, had had better opportunities to qualify themselves for membership. Opinions differed, too, as to the usefulness of the society. There were those who had been known to assail it violently as a glaring example of the very prejudice from which the colored race had suffered most ; and later, when such critics had succeeded in getting on the inside, they had been heard to maintain with zeal and earnestness that the society was a life-boat, an anchor, a bulwark and a shield, — a pillar of cloud by day and of fire by night, to guide their people through the social wilderness. Another alleged prerequisite for Blue Vein membership was that of free birth ; and while there was really no such requirement, it is doubtless true that very few of the members would have been unable to meet it if there had been. If there were one or two of the older members who had come up from the South and from slavery, their history presented enough romantic circumstances to rob their servile origin of its grosser aspects.

While there were no such tests of eligibility, it is true that the Blue Veins had their notions on these subjects, and that not all of them were equally liberal in regard to the things they collectively disclaimed. Mr. Ryder was one of the most conservative. Though he had not been among the founders of the society, but had come in some years later, his genius for social leadership was such that he had speedily become its recognized adviser and head, the custodian of its standards, and the preserver of its traditions. He shaped its social policy, was active in providing for its entertainment, and when the interest fell off, as it sometimes did, he fanned the embers until they burst again into a cheerful flame.

There were still other reasons for his popularity. While he was not as white as some of the Blue Veins, his appearance was such as to confer distinction upon them. His features were of a refined type, his hair was almost straight; he was always neatly dressed; his manners were irreproachable, and his morals above suspicion. He had come to Groveland a young man, and obtaining employment in the office of a railroad company as messenger had in time worked himself up to the position of stationery clerk, having charge of the distribution of the office supplies for the whole company. Although the lack of early training had hindered the orderly development of a naturally fine mind, it had not prevented him from doing a great deal of reading or from forming decidedly literary tastes. Poetry was his passion. He could repeat whole pages of the great English poets; and if his pronunciation was sometimes faulty, his eye, his voice, his gestures, would respond to the changing sentiment with a precision that revealed a poetic soul and disarmed criticism. He was economical, and had saved money; he owned and occupied a very comfortable house on a respectable street. His residence was handsomely furnished, containing among other things a good library, especially rich in poetry, a piano, and some

choice engravings. He generally shared his
house with some young couple, who looked
after his wants and were company for him;
for Mr. Ryder was a single man. In the
early days of his connection with the Blue
Veins he had been regarded as quite a catch,
and young ladies and their mothers had
manœuvred with much ingenuity to capture
him. Not, however, until Mrs. Molly Dixon
visited Groveland had any woman ever made
him wish to change his condition to that of a
married man.

Mrs. Dixon had come to Groveland from
Washington in the spring, and before the
summer was over she had won Mr. Ryder's
heart. She possessed many attractive quali-
ties. She was much younger than he; in
fact, he was old enough to have been her father, though no one knew exactly how old he
was. She was whiter than he, and better educated. She had moved in the best colored
society of the country, at Washington, and
had taught in the schools of that city. Such
a superior person had been eagerly welcomed
to the Blue Vein Society, and had taken a
leading part in its activities. Mr. Ryder had
at first been attracted by her charms of per-

son, for she was very good looking and not
over twenty-five; then by her refined manners and the vivacity of her wit. Her husband had been a government clerk, and at
his death had left a considerable life insur-
ance. She was visiting friends in Groveland,
and, finding the town and the people to her
liking, had prolonged her stay indefinitely.
She had not seemed displeased at Mr. Ryder's
attentions, but on the contrary had given
him every proper encouragement; indeed, a
younger and less cautious man would long
since have spoken. But he had made up his
mind, and had only to determine the time
when he would ask her to be his wife. He
decided to give a ball in her honor, and at
some time during the evening of the ball to
offer her his heart and hand. He had no
special fears about the outcome, but, with a
little touch of romance, he wanted the surroundings to be in harmony with his own
feelings when he should have received the
answer he expected.

Mr. Ryder resolved that this ball should
mark an epoch in the social history of Groveland. He knew, of course, — no one could
know better, — the entertainments that had

taken place in past years, and what must be
done to surpass them. His ball must be
worthy of the lady in whose honor it was to
be given, and must, by the quality of its
guests, set an example for the future. He
had observed of late a growing liberality,
almost a laxity, in social matters, even among
members of his own set, and had several times
been forced to meet in a social way persons
whose complexions and callings in life were
hardly up to the standard which he considered
proper for the society to maintain. He had a
theory of his own.

"I have no race prejudice," he would say,
"but we people of mixed blood are ground
between the upper and the nether millstone.
Our fate lies between absorption by the white
race and extinction in the black. The one
does n't want us yet, but may take us in time.
The other would welcome us, but it would be
for us a backward step. 'With malice towards none, with charity for all,' we must do
the best we can for ourselves and those who
are to follow us. Self-preservation is the first
law of nature."

His ball would serve by its exclusiveness to
counteract leveling tendencies, and his mar-

riage with Mrs. Dixon would help to further
the upward process of absorption he had been
wishing and waiting for.

II

The ball was to take place on Friday night.
The house had been put in order, the carpets
covered with canvas, the halls and stairs decorated with palms and potted plants ; and in
the afternoon Mr. Ryder sat on his front
porch, which the shade of a vine running up
over a wire netting made a cool and pleasant
lounging place. He expected to respond to
the toast " The Ladies " at the supper, and
from a volume of Tennyson — his favorite
poet — was fortifying himself with apt quo-
tations. The volume was open at " A Dream
of Fair Women." His eyes fell on these lines,
and he read them aloud to judge better of
their effect : —

> " At length I saw a lady within call,
>   Stiller than chisell'd marble, standing there ;
> A daughter of the gods, divinely tall,
>   And most divinely fair."

He marked the verse, and turning the page
read the stanza beginning, —

> " O sweet pale Margaret,
>   O rare pale Margaret."

He weighed the passage a moment, and decided that it would not do. Mrs. Dixon was the palest lady he expected at the ball, and she was of a rather ruddy complexion, and of lively disposition and buxom build. So he ran over the leaves until his eye rested on the description of Queen Guinevere : —

> "She seem'd a part of joyous Spring :
> A gown of grass-green silk she wore,
> Buckled with golden clasps before ;
> A light-green tuft of plumes she bore
> Closed in a golden ring.
>
> .   .   .   .   .   .
>
> "She look'd so lovely, as she sway'd
> The rein with dainty finger-tips,
> A man had given all other bliss,
> And all his worldly worth for this,
> To waste his whole heart in one kiss
> Upon her perfect lips."

As Mr. Ryder murmured these words audibly, with an appreciative thrill, he heard the latch of his gate click, and a light footfall sounding on the steps. He turned his head, and saw a woman standing before his door.

She was a little woman, not five feet tall, and proportioned to her height. Although she stood erect, and looked around her with very bright and restless eyes, she seemed

quite old; for her face was crossed and re-
crossed with a hundred wrinkles, and around
the edges of her bonnet could be seen pro-
truding here and there a tuft of short gray
wool.   She wore a blue calico gown of
ancient cut, a little red shawl fastened around
her shoulders with an old-fashioned brass
brooch, and a large bonnet profusely orna-
mented with faded red and yellow artificial
flowers.   And she was very black, — so black
that her toothless gums, revealed when she
opened her mouth to speak, were not red, but
blue.   She looked like a bit of the old plantation life, summoned up from the past by
the wave of a magician's wand, as the poet's
fancy had called into being the gracious
shapes of which Mr. Ryder had just been
reading.

He rose from his chair and came over to
where she stood.

"Good-afternoon, madam," he said.

"Good-evenin', suh," she answered, duck-
ing suddenly with a quaint curtsy.   Her
voice was shrill and piping, but softened
somewhat by age.   "Is dis yere whar Mistuh
Ryduh lib, suh?" she asked, looking around
her doubtfully, and glancing into the open

windows, through which some of the preparations for the evening were visible.

" Yes," he replied, with an air of kindly patronage, unconsciously flattered by her manner, " I am Mr. Ryder. Did you want to see me ? "

" Yas, suh, ef I ain't 'sturbin' of you too much."

"Not at all. Have a seat over here behind the vine, where it is cool. What can I do for you ? "

" 'Scuse me, suh," she continued, when she had sat down on the edge of a chair, " 'scuse me, suh, I 's lookin' for my husban'. I heerd you wuz a big man an' had libbed heah a long time, an' I 'lowed you would n't min' ef I 'd come roun' an' ax you ef you 'd ever heerd of a merlatter man by de name er Sam Taylor 'quirin' roun' in de chu'ches ermongs' de people fer his wife 'Liza Jane ? "

Mr. Ryder seemed to think for a moment.

" There used to be many such cases right after the war," he said, " but it has been so long that I have forgotten them. There are very few now. But tell me your story, and it may refresh my memory."

She sat back farther in her chair so as to

be more comfortable, and folded her withered hands in her lap.

"My name's 'Liza," she began, "'Liza Jane. W'en I wuz young I us'ter b'long ter Marse Bob Smif, down in ole Missoura. I wuz bawn down dere. W'en I wuz a gal I wuz married ter a man named Jim. But Jim died, an' after dat I married a merlatter man named Sam Taylor. Sam wuz free-bawn, but his mammy and daddy died, an' de w'ite folks 'prenticed him ter my marster fer ter work fer 'im 'tel he wuz growed up. Sam worked in de fiel', an' I wuz de cook. One day Ma'y Ann, ole miss's maid, came rushin' out ter de kitchen, an' says she, ''Liza Jane, ole marse gwine sell yo' Sam down de ribber.'

"'Go way f'm yere,' says I; 'my husban''s free!'

"'Don' make no diff'ence. I heerd ole marse tell ole miss he wuz gwine take yo' Sam 'way wid 'im ter-morrow, fer he needed money, an' he knowed whar he could git a t'ousan' dollars fer Sam an' no questions axed.'

"W'en Sam come home f'm de fiel' dat night, I tole him 'bout ole marse gwine

steal 'im, an' Sam run erway. His time wuz
mos' up, an' he swo' dat w'en he wuz twenty-
one he would come back an' he'p me run
erway, er else save up de money ter buy my
freedom. An' I know he'd 'a' done it, fer
he thought a heap er me, Sam did. But w'en
he come back he did n' fin' me, fer I wuz n'
dere. Ole marse had heerd dat I warned
Sam, so he had me whip' an' sol' down de
ribber.

"Den de wah broke out, an' w'en it wuz
ober de cullud folks wuz scattered. I went
back ter de ole home ; but Sam wuz n' dere,
an' I could n' l'arn nuffin' 'bout 'im. But I
knowed he'd be'n dere to look fer me an'
had n' foun' me, an' had gone erway ter hunt
fer me.

"I's be'n lookin' fer 'im eber sence," she
added simply, as though twenty-five years
were but a couple of weeks, "an' I knows
he's be'n lookin' fer me. Fer he sot a heap
er sto' by me, Sam did, an' I know he's be'n
huntin' fer me all dese years, — 'less'n he's
be'n sick er sump'n, so he could n' work, er
out'n his head, so he could n' 'member his
promise. I went back down de ribber, fer I
'lowed he'd gone down dere lookin' fer me.

I's be'n ter Noo Orleens, an' Atlanty, an'
Charleston, an' Richmon'; an' w'en I'd be'n
all ober de Souf I come ter de Norf. Fer I
knows I'll fin' 'im some er dese days," she
added softly, " er he'll fin' me, an' den we'll
bofe be as happy in freedom as we wuz in de
ole days befo' de wah." A smile stole over
her withered countenance as she paused a moment, and her bright eyes softened into a far-
away look.

This was the substance of the old woman's
story. She had wandered a little here and
there. Mr. Ryder was looking at her curiously when she finished.

"How have you lived all these years?" he
asked.

"Cookin', suh. I's a good cook. Does
you know anybody w'at needs a good cook,
suh? I's stoppin' wid a cullud fam'ly roun'
de corner yonder 'tel I kin git a place."

"Do you really expect to find your husband? He may be dead long ago."

She shook her head emphatically. " Oh
no, he ain' dead. De signs an' de tokens tells
me. I dremp three nights runnin' on'y dis las'
week dat I foun' him."

"He may have married another woman.

Your slave marriage would not have prevented him, for you never lived with him after the war, and without that your marriage does n't count."

"Would n' make no diff'ence wid Sam. He would n' marry no yuther 'ooman 'tel he foun' out 'bout me. I knows it," she added. "Sump'n 's be'n tellin' me all dese years dat I 's gwine fin' Sam 'fo' I dies."

"Perhaps he 's outgrown you, and climbed up in the world where he would n't care to have you find him."

"No, indeed, suh," she replied, "Sam ain' dat kin' er man. He wuz good ter me, Sam wuz, but he wuz n' much good ter nobody e'se, fer he wuz one er de triflin'es' han's on de plantation. I 'spec's ter haf ter suppo't 'im w'en I fin' 'im, fer he nebber would work 'less'n he had ter. But den he wuz free, an' he did n' git no pay fer his work, an' I don' blame 'im much. Mebbe he 's done better sence he run erway, but I ain' 'spectin' much."

"You may have passed him on the street a hundred times during the twenty-five years, and not have known him; time works great changes."

She smiled incredulously. "I 'd know 'im

'mongs' a hund'ed men. Fer dey wuz n' no yuther merlatter man like my man Sam, an' I could n' be mistook. I 's toted his picture roun' wid me twenty-five years."

"May I see it?" asked Mr. Ryder. "It might help me to remember whether I have seen the original."

As she drew a small parcel from her bosom he saw that it was fastened to a string that went around her neck. Removing several wrappers, she brought to light an old-fashioned daguerreotype in a black case. He looked long and intently at the portrait. It was faded with time, but the features were still distinct, and it was easy to see what manner of man it had represented.

He closed the case, and with a slow movement handed it back to her.

"I don't know of any man in town who goes by that name," he said, "nor have I heard of any one making such inquiries. But if you will leave me your address, I will give the matter some attention, and if I find out anything I will let you know."

She gave him the number of a house in the neighborhood, and went away, after thanking him warmly.

He wrote the address on the fly-leaf of
the volume of Tennyson, and, when she had
gone, rose to his feet and stood looking after
her curiously. As she walked down the street
with mincing step, he saw several persons
whom she passed turn and look back at her
with a smile of kindly amusement. When
she had turned the corner, he went upstairs
to his bedroom, and stood for a long time before the mirror of his dressing-case, gazing
thoughtfully at the reflection of his own face.

III

At eight o'clock the ballroom was a blaze
of light and the guests had begun to as-
semble; for there was a literary programme
and some routine business of the society to
be gone through with before the dancing.
A black servant in evening dress waited at
the door and directed the guests to the dress-
ing-rooms.

The occasion was long memorable among
the colored people of the city; not alone for
the dress and display, but for the high average of intelligence and culture that distinguished the gathering as a whole. There

were a number of school-teachers, several
young doctors, three or four lawyers, some
professional singers, an editor, a lieutenant
in the United States army spending his fur-
lough in the city, and others in various polite
callings; these were colored, though most of
them would not have attracted even a casual
glance because of any marked difference from
white people. Most of the ladies were in
evening costume, and dress coats and dancing pumps were the rule among the men. A
band of string music, stationed in an alcove
behind a row of palms, played popular airs
while the guests were gathering.

The dancing began at half past nine. At
eleven o'clock supper was served. Mr. Ryder
had left the ballroom some little time before
the intermission, but reappeared at the supper-
table. The spread was worthy of the occasion, and the guests did full justice to it.
When the coffee had been served, the toast-
master, Mr. Solomon Sadler, rapped for order.
He made a brief introductory speech, compli-
menting host and guests, and then presented
in their order the toasts of the evening. They
were responded to with a very fair display of
after-dinner wit.

" The last toast," said the toast-master,
when he reached the end of the list, " is one
which must appeal to us all. There is no one
of us of the sterner sex who is not at some
time dependent upon woman, — in infancy
for protection, in manhood for companionship, in old age for care and comforting. Our
good host has been trying to live alone, but
the fair faces I see around me to-night prove
that he too is largely dependent upon the
gentler sex for most that makes life worth
living, — the society and love of friends, —
and rumor is at fault if he does not soon yield
entire subjection to one of them. Mr. Ryder
will now respond to the toast, — The Ladies."

There was a pensive look in Mr. Ryder's
eyes as he took the floor and adjusted his eye-
glasses. He began by speaking of woman as
the gift of Heaven to man, and after some
general observations on the relations of the
sexes he said: " But perhaps the quality which
most distinguishes woman is her fidelity and
devotion to those she loves. History is full
of examples, but has recorded none more
striking than one which only to-day came
under my notice."

He then related, simply but effectively, the

story told by his visitor of the afternoon. He
gave it in the same soft dialect, which came
readily to his lips, while the company listened
attentively and sympathetically. For the
story had awakened a responsive thrill in
many hearts. There were some present who
had seen, and others who had heard their
fathers and grandfathers tell, the wrongs and
sufferings of this past generation, and all of
them still felt, in their darker moments, the
shadow hanging over them. Mr. Ryder went
on : —

"Such devotion and confidence are rare
even among women. There are many who
would have searched a year, some who would
have waited five years, a few who might
have hoped ten years; but for twenty-five
years this woman has retained her affection
for and her faith in a man she has not seen
or heard of in all that time.

" She came to me to-day in the hope that I
might be able to help her find this long-lost
husband. And when she was gone I gave my
fancy rein, and imagined a case I will put to
you.

"Suppose that this husband, soon after his
escape, had learned that his wife had been

sold away, and that such inquiries as he could make brought no information of her whereabouts. Suppose that he was young, and she much older than he; that he was light, and she was black; that their marriage was a slave marriage, and legally binding only if they chose to make it so after the war. Suppose, too, that he made his way to the North, as some of us have done, and there, where he had larger opportunities, had improved them, and had in the course of all these years grown to be as different from the ignorant boy who ran away from fear of slavery as the day is from the night. Suppose, even, that he had qualified himself, by industry, by thrift, and by study, to win the friendship and be considered worthy the society of such people as these I see around me to-night, gracing my board and filling my heart with gladness; for I am old enough to remember the day when such a gathering would not have been possible in this land. Suppose, too, that, as the years went by, this man's memory of the past grew more and more indistinct, until at last it was rarely, except in his dreams, that any image of this bygone period rose before his mind. And then suppose that accident

should bring to his knowledge the fact that
the wife of his youth, the wife he had left
behind him, — not one who had walked by
his side and kept pace with him in his upward
struggle, but one upon whom advancing
years and a laborious life had set their mark,
— was alive and seeking him, but that he
was absolutely safe from recognition or discovery, unless he chose to reveal himself.
My friends, what would the man do? I will
presume that he was one who loved honor,
and tried to deal justly with all men. I will
even carry the case further, and suppose that
perhaps he had set his heart upon another,
whom he had hoped to call his own. What
would he do, or rather what ought he to do,
in such a crisis of a lifetime?

" It seemed to me that he might hesitate,
and I imagined that I was an old friend, a
near friend, and that he had come to me for
advice ; and I argued the case with him. I
tried to discuss it impartially. After we had
looked upon the matter from every point of
view, I said to him, in words that we all
know : —

> ' This above all: to thine own self be true,
> And it must follow, as the night the day,
> Thou canst not then be false to any man.'

Then, finally, I put the question to him, ' Shall you acknowledge her ? '

" And now, ladies and gentlemen, friends and companions, I ask you, what should he have done ? "

There was something in Mr. Ryder's voice that stirred the hearts of those who sat around him. It suggested more than mere sympathy with an imaginary situation ; it seemed rather in the nature of a personal appeal. It was observed, too, that his look rested more especially upon Mrs. Dixon, with a mingled expression of renunciation and inquiry.

She had listened, with parted lips and streaming eyes. She was the first to speak : " He should have acknowledged her."

" Yes," they all echoed, " he should have acknowledged her."

" My friends and companions," responded Mr. Ryder, " I thank you, one and all. It is the answer I expected, for I knew your hearts."

He turned and walked toward the closed door of an adjoining room, while every eye followed him in wondering curiosity. He came back in a moment, leading by the hand his visitor of the afternoon, who stood startled and trembling at the sudden plunge into this scene of brilliant gayety. She was neatly dressed in gray, and wore the white cap of an elderly woman.

"Ladies and gentlemen," he said, "this is the woman, and I am the man, whose story I have told you. Permit me to introduce to you the wife of my youth."

HER VIRGINIA MAMMY

I

THE pianist had struck up a lively two-step, and soon the floor was covered with couples, each turning on its own axis, and all revolving around a common centre, in obedience perhaps to the same law of motion that governs the planetary systems. The dancing-hall was a long room, with a waxed floor that glistened with the reflection of the lights from the chandeliers. The walls were hung in paper of blue and white, above a varnished hard wood wainscoting; the monotony of surface being broken by numerous windows draped with curtains of dotted muslin, and by occasional engravings and colored pictures representing the dances of various nations, judiciously selected. The rows of chairs along the two sides of the room were left unoccupied by the time the music was well under way, for the pianist, a tall colored woman with long fingers and a muscular wrist, played

with a verve and a swing that set the feet of
the listeners involuntarily in motion.

The dance was sure to occupy the class for
a quarter of an hour at least, and the little
dancing-mistress took the opportunity to slip
away to her own sitting-room, which was on
the same floor of the block, for a few minutes
of rest. Her day had been a hard one.
There had been a matinée at two o'clock, a
children's class at four, and at eight o'clock
the class now on the floor had assembled.

When she reached the sitting-room she
gave a start of pleasure. A young man rose
at her entrance, and advanced with both
hands extended — a tall, broad-shouldered,
fair-haired young man, with a frank and
kindly countenance, now lit up with the ani-
mation of pleasure. He seemed about twenty-
six or twenty-seven years old. His face was
of the type one instinctively associates with
intellect and character, and it gave the impression, besides, of that intangible something which we call race. He was neatly
and carefully dressed, though his clothing was
not without indications that he found it necessary or expedient to practice economy.

"Good-evening, Clara," he said, taking her

hands in his; " I 've been waiting for you five minutes. I supposed you would be in, but if you had been a moment later I was going to the hall to look you up. You seem tired tonight," he added, drawing her nearer to him and scanning her features at short range. " This work is too hard ; you are not fitted for it. When are you going to give it up ? "

" The season is almost over," she answered, " and then I shall stop for the summer."

He drew her closer still and kissed her lovingly. " Tell me, Clara," he said, looking down into her face, — he was at least a foot taller than she, — " when I am to have my answer."

" Will you take the answer you can get tonight ? " she asked with a wan smile.

" I will take but one answer, Clara. But do not make me wait too long for that. Why, just think of it ! I have known you for six months."

" That is an extremely long time," said Clara, as they sat down side by side.

" It has been an age," he rejoined. " For a fortnight of it, too, which seems longer than all the rest, I have been waiting for my answer. I am turning gray under the suspense. Seriously, Clara dear, what shall it be? or rather, when shall it be? for to the other question there is but one answer possible."

He looked into her eyes, which slowly filled with tears. She repulsed him gently as he bent over to kiss them away.

"You know I love you, John, and why I do not say what you wish. You must give me a little more time to make up my mind before I can consent to burden you with a nameless wife, one who does not know who her mother was " —

" She was a good woman, and beautiful, if you are at all like her."

" Or her father " —

" He was a gentleman and a scholar, if you inherited from him your mind or your manners."

" It is good of you to say that, and I try to believe it. But it is a serious matter; it is a dreadful thing to have no name."

" You are known by a worthy one, which was freely given you, and is legally yours."

"I know — and I am grateful for it. After all, though, it is not my real name; and since I have learned that it was not, it seems like a garment — something external, accessory, and not a part of myself. It does not mean what one's own name would signify."

"Take mine, Clara, and make it yours; I lay it at your feet. Some honored men have borne it."

" Ah yes, and that is what makes my position the harder. Your great-grandfather was governor of Connecticut."

" I have heard my mother say so."

" And one of your ancestors came over in the Mayflower."

"In some capacity — I have never been quite clear whether as ship's cook or before the mast."

" Now you are insincere, John ; but you cannot deceive me. You never spoke in that way about your ancestors until you learned that I had none. I know you are proud of them, and that the memory of the governor and the judge and the Harvard professor and the Mayflower pilgrim makes you strive to excel, in order to prove yourself worthy of them."

" It did until I met you, Clara. Now the one inspiration of my life is the hope to make you mine."

" And your profession ? "

"It will furnish me the means to take you out of this; you are not fit for toil."

"And your book — your treatise that is to make you famous?"

"I have worked twice as hard on it and accomplished twice as much since I have hoped that you might share my success."

"Oh! if I but knew the truth!" she sighed, "or could find it out! I realize that I am absurd, that I ought to be happy. I love my parents — my foster-parents — dearly. I owe them everything. Mother — poor, dear mother! — could not have loved me better or cared for me more faithfully had I been her own child. Yet — I am ashamed to say it — I always felt that I was not like them, that there was a subtle difference between us. They were contented in prosperity, resigned in misfortune; I was ever restless, and filled with vague ambitions. They were good, but dull. They loved me, but they never said so. I feel that there is warmer, richer blood coursing in my veins than the placid stream that crept through theirs."

"There will never be any such people to me as they were," said her lover, "for they took you and brought you up for me."

"Sometimes," she went on dreamily, "I feel sure that I am of good family, and the blood of my ancestors seems to call to me in clear and certain tones. Then again when my mood changes, I am all at sea — I feel that even if I had but simply to turn my hand to learn who I am and whence I came, I should shrink from taking the step, for fear that what I might learn would leave me forever unhappy."

"Dearest," he said, taking her in his arms, while from the hall and down the corridor came the softened strains of music, "put aside these unwholesome fancies. Your past is shrouded in mystery. Take my name, as you have taken my love, and I'll make your future so happy that you won't have time to think of the past. What are a lot of musty, mouldy old grandfathers, compared with life and love and happiness? It's hardly good form to mention one's ancestors nowadays, and what's the use of them at all if one can't boast of them?"

"It's all very well of you to talk that way," she rejoined. "But suppose you should marry me, and when you become famous and rich, and patients flock to your office, and fashionable people to your home, and every one wants to know who you are and whence you came, you'll be obliged to bring out the governor, and the judge, and the rest of them. If you should refrain, in order to forestall embarrassing inquiries about *my* ancestry, I should have deprived you of something you are entitled to, something which has a real social value. And when people found out all about you, as they eventually would from some source, they would want to know — we Americans are a curious people — who your wife was, and you could only say " —

" The best and sweetest woman on earth, whom I love unspeakably."

" You know that is not what I mean. You could only say — a Miss Nobody, from Nowhere."

" A Miss Hohlfelder, from Cincinnati, the only child of worthy German parents, who fled from their own country in '49 to escape political persecution — an ancestry that one surely need not be ashamed of."

" No; but the consciousness that it was not true would be always with me, poisoning my mind, and darkening my life and yours."

" Your views of life are entirely too tragic,

Clara," the young man argued soothingly.
"We are all worms of the dust, and if we
go back far enough, each of us has had millions
of ancestors ; peasants and serfs, most of them ;
thieves, murderers, and vagabonds, many of
them, no doubt ; and therefore the best of us
have but little to boast of. Yet we are all
made after God's own image, and formed by
his hand, for his ends ; and therefore not to
be lightly despised, even the humblest of us,
least of all by ourselves. For the past we can
claim no credit, for those who made it died
with it. Our destiny lies in the future."

"Yes," she sighed, "I know all that. But
I am not like you. A woman is not like a
man ; she cannot lose herself in theories and
generalizations. And there are tests that even
all your philosophy could not endure. Suppose you should marry me, and then some
time, by the merest accident, you should learn
that my origin was the worst it could be —
that I not only had no name, but was not
entitled to one."

"I cannot believe it," he said, "and from
what we do know of your history it is hardly
possible. If I learned it, I should forget it,
unless, perchance, it should enhance your

value in my eyes, by stamping you as a rare
work of nature, an exception to the law of
heredity, a triumph of pure beauty and good-
ness over the grosser limitations of matter.
I cannot imagine, now that I know you,
anything that could make me love you less.
I would marry you just the same — even
if you were one of your dancing-class to-
night."

"I must go back to them," said Clara, as
the music ceased.

"My answer," he urged, "give me my
answer!"

"Not to-night, John," she pleaded. "Grant
me a little longer time to make up my mind
— for your sake."

"Not for my sake, Clara, no."

"Well — for mine." She let him take her
in his arms and kiss her again.

"I have a patient yet to see to-night," he
said as he went out. "If I am not detained
too long, I may come back this way — if I see
the lights in the hall still burning. Do not
wonder if I ask you again for my answer,
for I shall be unhappy until I get it."

II

A stranger entering the hall with Miss
Hohlfelder would have seen, at first glance,
only a company of well-dressed people, with
nothing to specially distinguish them from
ordinary humanity in temperate climates.
After the eye had rested for a moment and
begun to separate the mass into its compo-
nent parts, one or two dark faces would
have arrested its attention ; and with the suggestion thus offered, a closer inspection would
have revealed that they were nearly all a
little less than white. With most of them
this fact would not have been noticed, while
they were alone or in company with one another, though if a fair white person had gone
among them it would perhaps have been more
apparent. From the few who were undis-
tinguishable from pure white, the colors ran
down the scale by minute gradations to the
two or three brown faces at the other ex-
tremity.

It was Miss Hohlfelder's first colored class.
She had been somewhat startled when first
asked to take it. No person of color had ever
applied to her for lessons ; and while a woman

of that race had played the piano for her for several months, she had never thought of colored people as possible pupils. So when she was asked if she would take a class of twenty or thirty, she had hesitated, and begged for time to consider the application. She knew that several of the more fashionable dancing-schools tabooed all pupils, singly or in classes, who labored under social disabilities — and this included the people of at least one other race who were vastly farther along in the world than the colored people of the community where Miss Hohlfelder lived. Personally she had no such prejudice, except perhaps a little shrinking at the thought of personal contact with the dark faces of whom Americans always think when " colored people " are spoken of. Again, a class of forty pupils was not to be despised, for she taught for money, which was equally current and desirable, regardless of its color. She had consulted her foster-parents, and after them her lover. Her foster-parents, who were German-born, and had never become thoroughly Americanized, saw no objection. As for her lover, he was indifferent.

" Do as you please," he said. " It may

drive away some other pupils. If it should break up the business entirely, perhaps you might be willing to give me a chance so much the sooner."

She mentioned the matter to one or two other friends, who expressed conflicting opinions. She decided at length to take the class, and take the consequences.

"I don't think it would be either right or kind to refuse them for any such reason, and I don't believe I shall lose anything by it."

She was somewhat surprised, and pleasantly so, when her class came together for their first lesson, at not finding them darker and more uncouth. Her pupils were mostly people whom she would have passed on the street without a second glance, and among them were several whom she had known by sight for years, but had never dreamed of as being colored people. Their manners were good, they dressed quietly and as a rule with good taste, avoiding rather than choosing bright colors and striking combinations — whether from natural preference, or because of a slightly morbid shrinking from criticism, of course she could not say. Among them, the dancing-mistress soon learned, there were law-

yers and doctors, teachers, telegraph operators,
clerks, milliners and dressmakers, students of
the local college and scientific school, and,
somewhat to her awe at the first meeting,
even a member of the legislature. They were
mostly young, although a few light - hearted
older people joined the class, as much for
company as for the dancing.

"Of course, Miss Hohlfelder," explained
Mr. Solomon Sadler, to whom the teacher had
paid a compliment on the quality of the class,
"the more advanced of us are not numerous
enough to make the fine distinctions that are
possible among white people ; and of course
as we rise in life we can't get entirely away
from our brothers and our sisters and our
cousins, who don't always keep abreast of us.
We do, however, draw certain lines of character and manners and occupation. You see
the sort of people we are. Of course we have
no prejudice against color, and we regard all
labor as honorable, provided a man does the
best he can. But we must have standards
that will give our people something to
aspire to."

The class was not a difficult one, as many
of the members were already fairly good

dancers. Indeed the class had been formed as much for pleasure as for instruction. Music and hall rent and a knowledge of the latest dances could be obtained cheaper in this way than in any other. The pupils had made rapid progress, displaying in fact a natural aptitude for rhythmic motion, and a keen susceptibility to musical sounds. As their race had never been criticised for these characteristics, they gave them full play, and soon developed, most of them, into graceful and indefatigable dancers. They were now almost at the end of their course, and this was the evening of the last lesson but one.

Miss Hohlfelder had remarked to her lover more than once that it was a pleasure to teach them. "They enter into the spirit of it so thoroughly, and they seem to enjoy themselves so much."

"One would think," he suggested, "that the whitest of them would find their position painful and more or less pathetic; to be so white and yet to be classed as black — so near and yet so far."

"They don't accept our classification blindly. They do not acknowledge any inferiority; they think they are a great deal

better than any but the best white people,"
replied Miss Hohlfelder. "And since they
have been coming here, do you know," she
went on, "I hardly think of them as any different from other people. I feel perfectly at
home among them."

"It is a great thing to have faith in one's
self," he replied. "It is a fine thing, too, to
be able to enjoy the passing moment. One of
your greatest charms in my eyes, Clara, is that
in your lighter moods you have this faculty.
You sing because you love to sing. You find
pleasure in dancing, even by way of work.
You feel the *joi de vivre* — the joy of living.
You are not always so, but when you are so
I think you most delightful."

Miss Hohlfelder, upon entering the hall,
spoke to the pianist and then exchanged a few
words with various members of the class.
The pianist began to play a dreamy Strauss
waltz. When the dance was well under way
Miss Hohlfelder left the hall again and
stepped into the ladies' dressing - room.
There was a woman seated quietly on a couch
in a corner, her hands folded on her lap.

"Good-evening, Miss Hohlfelder. You
do not seem as bright as usual to-night."

Miss Hohlfelder felt a sudden yearning for sympathy. Perhaps it was the gentle tones of the greeting; perhaps the kindly expression of the soft though faded eyes that were scanning Miss Hohlfelder's features. The woman was of the indefinite age between forty and fifty. There were lines on her face which, if due to years, might have carried her even past the half-century mark, but if caused by trouble or ill health might leave her somewhat below it. She was quietly dressed in black, and wore her slightly wavy hair low over her ears, where it lay naturally in the ripples which some others of her sex so sedulously seek by art. A little woman, of clear olive complexion and regular features, her face was almost a perfect oval, except as time had marred its outline. She had been in the habit of coming to the class with some young women of the family she lived with, part boarder, part seamstress and friend of the family. Sometimes, while waiting for her young charges, the music would jar her nerves, and she would seek the comparative quiet of the dressing-room.

"Oh, I'm all right, Mrs. Harper," replied the dancing-mistress, with a brave attempt at cheerfulness, — "just a little tired, after a hard day's work."

She sat down on the couch by the elder woman's side. Mrs. Harper took her hand and stroked it gently, and Clara felt soothed and quieted by her touch.

"There are tears in your eyes and trouble in your face. I know it, for I have shed the one and known the other. Tell me, child, what ails you? I am older than you, and perhaps I have learned some things in the hard school of life that may be of comfort or service to you."

Such a request, coming from a comparative stranger, might very properly have been resented or lightly parried. But Clara was not what would be called self-contained. Her griefs seemed lighter when they were shared with others, even in spirit. There was in her nature a childish strain that craved sympathy and comforting. She had never known — or if so it was only in a dim and dreamlike past — the tender, brooding care that was her conception of a mother's love. Mrs. Hohlfelder had been fond of her in a placid way, and had given her every comfort and luxury her means permitted. Clara's

ideal of maternal love had been of another
and more romantic type; she had thought of
a fond, impulsive mother, to whose bosom
she could fly when in trouble or distress, and
to whom she could communicate her sorrows
and trials; who would dry her tears and
soothe her with caresses. Now, when even
her kind foster-mother was gone, she felt still
more the need of sympathy and companionship with her own sex; and when this little
Mrs. Harper spoke to her so gently, she felt
her heart respond instinctively.

"Yes, Mrs. Harper," replied Clara with a
sigh, "I am in trouble, but it is trouble that
you nor any one else can heal."

"You do not know, child. A simple
remedy can sometimes cure a very grave
complaint. Tell me your trouble, if it is
something you are at liberty to tell."

"I have a story," said Clara, "and it is a
strange one, — a story I have told to but one
other person, one very dear to me."

"He must be dear to you indeed, from the
tone in which you speak of him. Your very
accents breathe love."

"Yes, I love him, and if you saw him —
perhaps you have seen him, for he has looked

in here once or twice during the dancing-
lessons — you would know why I love him.
He is handsome, he is learned, he is ambitious,
he is brave, he is good; he is poor, but he
will not always be so; and he loves me, oh, so
much!"

The other woman smiled. "It is not so
strange to love, nor yet to be loved. And
all lovers are handsome and brave and fond."

"That is not all of my story. He wants
to marry me." Clara paused, as if to let this
statement impress itself upon the other.

"True lovers always do," said the elder
woman.

"But sometimes, you know, there are circumstances which prevent them."

"Ah yes," murmured the other reflectively, and looking at the girl with deeper
interest, "circumstances which prevent them.
I have known of such a case."

"The circumstance which prevents us from
marrying is my story."

"Tell me your story, child, and perhaps, if
I cannot help you otherwise, I can tell you
one that will make yours seem less sad."

"You know me," said the young woman,
"as Miss Hohlfelder; but that is not actu-

ally my name. In fact I do not know my
real name, for I am not the daughter of Mr.
and Mrs. Hohlfelder, but only an adopted
child. While Mrs. Hohlfelder lived, I never
knew that I was not her child. I knew I was
very different from her and father, — I mean
Mr. Hohlfelder. I knew they were fair and
I was dark; they were stout and I was slender; they were slow and I was quick. But
of course I never dreamed of the true reason
of this difference. When mother — Mrs.
Hohlfelder — died, I found among her things
one day a little packet, carefully wrapped up,
containing a child's slip and some trinkets.
The paper wrapper of the packet bore an in-
scription that awakened my curiosity. I
asked father Hohlfelder whose the things had
been, and then for the first time I learned
my real story.

"I was not their own daughter, he stated,
but an adopted child. Twenty-three years
ago, when he had lived in St. Louis, a steamboat explosion had occurred up the river, and
on a piece of wreckage floating down stream,
a girl baby had been found. There was
nothing on the child to give a hint of its
home or parentage; and no one came to claim

it, though the fact that a child had been
found was advertised all along the river.
It was believed that the infant's parents must
have perished in the wreck, and certainly no
one of those who were saved could identify
the child.   There had been a passenger list
on board the steamer, but the list, with the
officer who kept it, had been lost in the accident.   The child was turned over to an orphan asylum, from which within a year it
was adopted by the two kind-hearted and
childless German people who brought it up
as their own.   I was that child."

The woman seated by Clara's side had
listened with strained attention.   "Did you
learn the name of the steamboat?" she asked
quietly, but quickly, when Clara paused.

"The Pride of St. Louis," answered Clara.
She did not look at Mrs. Harper, but was
gazing dreamily toward the front, and therefore did not see the expression that sprang
into the other's face, — a look in which hope
struggled with fear, and yearning love with
both, — nor the strong effort with which
Mrs. Harper controlled herself and moved not
one muscle while the other went on.

"I was never sought," Clara continued,

"and the good people who brought me up gave me every care. Father and mother — I can never train my tongue to call them anything else — were very good to me. When they adopted me they were poor; he was a pharmacist with a small shop. Later on he moved to Cincinnati, where he made and sold a popular 'patent' medicine and amassed a fortune. Then I went to a fashionable school, was taught French, and deportment, and dancing. Father Hohlfelder made some bad investments, and lost most of his money. The patent medicine fell off in popularity. A year or two ago we came to this city to live. Father bought this block and opened the little drug store below. We moved into the rooms upstairs. The business was poor, and I felt that I ought to do something to earn money and help support the family. I could dance; we had this hall, and it was not rented all the time, so I opened a dancing-school."

"Tell me, child," said the other woman, with restrained eagerness, "what were the things found upon you when you were taken from the river?"

"Yes," answered the girl, "I will. But I have not told you all my story, for this is but the prelude. About a year ago a young doctor rented an office in our block. We met each other, at first only now and then, and afterwards oftener; and six months ago he told me that he loved me."

She paused, and sat with half opened lips and dreamy eyes, looking back into the past six months.

"And the things found upon you" —

"Yes, I will show them to you when you have heard all my story. He wanted to marry me, and has asked me every week since. I have told him that I love him, but I have not said I would marry him. I don't think it would be right for me to do so, unless I could clear up this mystery. I believe he is going to be great and rich and famous, and there might come a time when he would be ashamed of me. I don't say that I shall never marry him; for I have hoped — I have a presentiment that in some strange way I shall find out who I am, and who my parents were. It may be mere imagination on my part, but somehow I believe it is more than that."

"Are you sure there was no mark on the things that were found upon you?" said the elder woman.

" Ah yes," sighed Clara, " I am sure, for I
have looked at them a hundred times. They
tell me nothing, and yet they suggest to me
many things. Come," she said, taking the
other by the hand, " and I will show them
to you."

She led the way along the hall to her sitting-room, and to her bedchamber beyond.
It was a small room hung with paper showing a
pattern of morning-glories on a light ground,
with dotted muslin curtains, a white iron bed-
stead, a few prints on the wall, a rocking-
chair — a very dainty room. She went to
the maple dressing-case, and opened one of
the drawers.

As they stood for a moment, the mirror re-
flecting and framing their image, more
than one point of resemblance between them
was emphasized. There was something of
the same oval face, and in Clara's hair a faint
suggestion of the wave in the older woman's ; and though Clara was fairer of complexion, and her eyes were gray and the
other's black, there was visible, under the influence of the momentary excitement, one of
those indefinable likenesses which are at times
encountered, — sometimes marking blood re-

lationship, sometimes the impress of a common training; in one case perhaps a mere earmark of temperament, and in another the index of a type. Except for the difference in color, one might imagine that if the younger woman were twenty years older the resemblance would be still more apparent.

Clara reached her hand into the drawer and drew out a folded packet, which she unwrapped, Mrs. Harper following her movements meanwhile with a suppressed intensity of interest which Clara, had she not been absorbed in her own thoughts, could not have failed to observe.

When the last fold of paper was removed there lay revealed a child's muslin slip. Clara lifted it and shook it gently until it was unfolded before their eyes. The lower half was delicately worked in a lacelike pattern, revealing an immense amount of patient labor.

The elder woman seized the slip with hands which could not disguise their trembling. Scanning the garment carefully, she seemed to be noting the pattern of the needlework, and then, pointing to a certain spot, exclaimed : —

" I thought so ! I was sure of it ! Do you
not see the letters — M. S. ? "

" Oh, how wonderful ! " Clara seized the
slip in turn and scanned the monogram.
" How strange that you should see that at once
and that I should not have discovered it,
who have looked at it a hundred times ! And
here," she added, opening a small pack-
age which had been inclosed in the other,
" is my coral necklace. Perhaps your keen
eyes can find something in that."

It was a simple trinket, at which the older
woman gave but a glance — a glance that
added to her emotion.

" Listen, child," she said, laying her trembling hand on the other's arm. " It is all
very strange and wonderful, for that slip and
necklace, and, now that I have seen them,
your face and your voice and your ways, all
tell me who you are. Your eyes are your
father's eyes, your voice is your father's voice.
The slip was worked by your mother's hand."

" Oh ! " cried Clara, and for a moment the
whole world swam before her eyes.

" I was on the Pride of St. Louis, and I
knew your father — and your mother."

Clara, pale with excitement, burst into tears,

and would have fallen had not the other woman caught her in her arms. Mrs. Harper
placed her on the couch, and, seated by her
side, supported her head on her shoulder.
Her hands seemed to caress the young woman
with every touch.

"Tell me, oh, tell me all!" Clara demanded, when the first wave of emotion had
subsided. "Who were my father and my
mother, and who am I?"

The elder woman restrained her emotion
with an effort, and answered as composedly as
she could, —

"There were several hundred passengers on
the Pride of St. Louis when she left Cincinnati on that fateful day, on her regular trip
to New Orleans. Your father and mother
were on the boat — and I was on the boat.
We were going down the river, to take ship
at New Orleans for France, a country which
your father loved."

"Who was my father?" asked Clara. The
woman's words fell upon her ear like water
on a thirsty soil.

"Your father was a Virginia gentleman,
and belonged to one of the first families,
the Staffords, of Melton County."

Clara drew herself up unconsciously, and into her face there came a frank expression of pride which became it wonderfully, setting off a beauty that needed only this to make it all but perfect of its type.

"I knew it must be so," she murmured. "I have often felt it. Blood will always tell. And my mother?"

"Your mother — also belonged to one of the first families of Virginia, and in her veins flowed some of the best blood of the Old Dominion."

"What was her maiden name?"

"Mary Fairfax. As I was saying, your father was a Virginia gentleman. He was as handsome a man as ever lived, and proud, oh, so proud! — and good, and kind. He was a graduate of the University and had studied abroad."

"My mother — was she beautiful?"

"She was much admired, and your father loved her from the moment he first saw her. Your father came back from Europe, upon his father's sudden death, and entered upon his inheritance. But he had been away from Virginia so long, and had read so many books, that he had outgrown his home. He did not

believe that slavery was right, and one of the
first things he did was to free his slaves.
His views were not popular, and he sold out
his lands a year before the war, with the intention of moving to Europe."

" In the mean time he had met and loved
and married my mother?"

" In the mean time he had met and loved
your mother."

" My mother was a Virginia belle, was she
not?"

" The Fairfaxes," answered Mrs. Harper,
" were the first of the first families, the bluest
of the blue-bloods. The Miss Fairfaxes were
all beautiful and all social favorites."

" What did my father do then, when he
had sold out in Virginia?"

" He went with your mother and you — you
were then just a year old — to Cincinnati,
to settle up some business connected with
his estate. When he had completed his
business, he embarked on the Pride of St.
Louis with you and your mother and a colored
nurse."

" And how did you know about them?"
asked Clara.

" I was one of the party.   I was " —

"You were the colored nurse? — my 'mammy,' they would have called you in my old Virginia home?"

"Yes, child, I was — your mammy. Upon my bosom you have rested; my breasts once gave you nourishment; my hands once ministered to you; my arms sheltered you, and my heart loved you and mourned you like a mother loves and mourns her firstborn."

"Oh, how strange, how delightful!" exclaimed Clara. "Now I understand why you clasped me so tightly, and were so agitated when I told you my story. It is too good for me to believe. I am of good blood, of an old and aristocratic family. My presentiment has come true. I can marry my lover, and I shall owe all my happiness to you. How can I ever repay you?"

"You can kiss me, child, kiss your mammy."

Their lips met, and they were clasped in each other's arms. One put into the embrace all of her new-found joy, the other all the suppressed feeling of the last half hour, which in turn embodied the unsatisfied yearning of many years.

The music had ceased and the pupils had

left the hall.   Mrs. Harper's charges had supposed her gone, and had left for home without her.   But the two women, sitting in Clara's chamber, hand in hand, were oblivious to external things and noticed neither the hour nor the cessation of the music.

"Why, dear mammy," said the young woman musingly, "did you not find me, and restore me to my people?"

"Alas, child! I was not white, and when I was picked up from the water, after floating miles down the river, the man who found me kept me prisoner for a time, and, there being no inquiry for me, pretended not to believe that I was free, and took me down to New Orleans and sold me as a slave.   A few years later the war set me free.   I went to St. Louis but could find no trace of you.   I had hardly dared to hope that a child had been saved, when so many grown men and women had lost their lives.   I made such inquiries as I could, but all in vain."

"Did you go to the orphan asylum?"

"The orphan asylum had been burned and with it all the records.   The war had scattered the people so that I could find no one who knew about a lost child saved from a river wreck. There were many orphans in those days, and one more or less was not likely to dwell in the public mind."

" Did you tell my people in Virginia ? "

" They, too, were scattered by the war. Your uncles lost their lives on the battlefield. The family mansion was burned to the ground. Your father's remaining relatives were reduced to poverty, and moved away from Virginia."

" What of my mother's people ? "

" They are all dead. God punished them. They did not love your father, and did not wish him to marry your mother. They helped to drive him to his death."

" I am alone in the world, then, without kith or kin," murmured Clara, " and yet, strange to say, I am happy. If I had known my people and lost them, I should be sad. They are gone, but they have left me their name and their blood. I would weep for my poor father and mother if I were not so glad."

Just then some one struck a chord upon the piano in the hall, and the sudden breaking of the stillness recalled Clara's attention to the lateness of the hour.

" I had forgotten about the class," she exclaimed. " I must go and attend to them."

They walked along the corridor and entered the hall. Dr. Winthrop was seated at the piano, drumming idly on the keys.

" I did not know where you had gone," he said. " I knew you would be around, of course, since the lights were not out, and so I came in here to wait for you."

" Listen, John, I have a wonderful story to tell you."

Then she told him Mrs. Harper's story. He listened attentively and sympathetically, at certain points taking his eyes from Clara's face and glancing keenly at Mrs. Harper, who was listening intently. As he looked from one to the other he noticed the resemblance between them, and something in his expression caused Mrs. Harper's eyes to fall, and then glance up appealingly.

" And now," said Clara, " I am happy. I know my name. I am a Virginia Stafford. I belong to one, yes, to two of what were the first families of Virginia. John, my family is as good as yours. If I remember my history correctly, the Cavaliers looked down upon the Roundheads."

" I admit my inferiority," he replied. " If you are happy I am glad."

" Clara Stafford," mused the girl. " It is a pretty name."

" You will never have to use it," her lover declared, " for now you will take mine."

" Then I shall have nothing left of all that I have found " —

" Except your husband," asserted Dr. Winthrop, putting his arm around her, with an air of assured possession.

Mrs. Harper was looking at them with moistened eyes in which joy and sorrow, love and gratitude, were strangely blended. Clara put out her hand to her impulsively.

" And my mammy," she cried, " my dear Virginia mammy."

THE SHERIFF'S CHILDREN

BRANSON COUNTY, North Carolina, is in a
sequestered district of one of the staidest
and most conservative States of the Union.
Society in Branson County is almost primitive
in its simplicity.   Most of the white people
own the farms they till, and even before the
war there were no very wealthy families to
force their neighbors, by comparison, into the
category of "poor whites."

To Branson County, as to most rural com-
munities in the South, the war is the one historical event that overshadows all others.   It
is the era from which all local chronicles
are dated, — births, deaths, marriages, storms,
freshets.   No description of the life of any
Southern community would be perfect that
failed to emphasize the all pervading influence of the great conflict.

Yet the fierce tide of war that had
rushed through the cities and along the great
highways of the country had comparatively

speaking but slightly disturbed the sluggish current of life in this region, remote from railroads and navigable streams. To the north in Virginia, to the west in Tennessee, and all along the seaboard the war had raged ; but the thunder of its cannon had not disturbed the echoes of Branson County, where the loudest sounds heard were the crack of some hunter's rifle, the baying of some deep-mouthed hound, or the yodel of some tuneful negro on his way through the pine forest. To the east, Sherman's army had passed on its march to the sea ; but no straggling band of "bummers" had penetrated the confines of Branson County. The war, it is true, had robbed the county of the flower of its young manhood ; but the burden of taxation, the doubt and uncertainty of the conflict, and the sting of ultimate defeat, had been borne by the people with an apathy that robbed misfortune of half its sharpness.

The nearest approach to town life afforded by Branson County is found in the little village of Troy, the county seat, a hamlet with a population of four or five hundred.

Ten years make little difference in the appearance of these remote Southern towns.

If a railroad is built through one of them, it infuses some enterprise; the social corpse is galvanized by the fresh blood of civilization that pulses along the farthest ramifications of our great system of commercial highways. At the period of which I write, no railroad had come to Troy. If a traveler, accustomed to the bustling life of cities, could have ridden through Troy on a summer day, he might easily have fancied himself in a deserted village. Around him he would have seen weather-beaten houses, innocent of paint, the shingled roofs in many instances covered with a rich growth of moss. Here and there he would have met a razor-backed hog lazily rooting his way along the principal thoroughfare; and more than once be would probably have had to disturb the slumbers of some yellow dog, dozing away the hours in the ardent sunshine, and reluctantly yielding up his place in the middle of the dusty road.

On Saturdays the village presented a somewhat livelier appearance, and the shade trees around the court house square and along Front Street served as hitching-posts for a goodly number of horses and mules and stunted oxen, belonging to the farmer-folk who had come in to trade at the two or three local stores.

A murder was a rare event in Branson County. Every well-informed citizen could tell the number of homicides committed in the county for fifty years back, and whether the slayer, in any given instance, had escaped, either by flight or acquittal, or had suffered the penalty of the law. So, when it became known in Troy early one Friday morning in summer, about ten years after the war, that old Captain Walker, who had served in Mexico under Scott, and had left an arm on the field of Gettysburg, had been foully murdered during the night, there was intense excitement in the village. Business was practically suspended, and the citizens gathered in little groups to discuss the murder, and speculate upon the identity of the murderer. It transpired from testimony at the coroner's inquest, held during the morning, that a strange mulatto had been seen going in the direction of Captain Walker's house the night before, and had been met going away from Troy early Friday morning, by a farmer on his way to town. Other circumstances seemed to connect the stranger with the crime. The sheriff organized a posse to search for him, and early in the evening, when most of the citizens of Troy were at supper, the suspected man was brought in and lodged in the county jail.

By the following morning the news of the capture had spread to the farthest limits of the county. A much larger number of people than usual came to town that Saturday, — bearded men in straw hats and blue homespun shirts, and butternut trousers of great amplitude of material and vagueness of outline; women in homespun frocks and slat-bonnets, with faces as expressionless as the dreary sandhills which gave them a meagre sustenance.

The murder was almost the sole topic of conversation. A steady stream of curious observers visited the house of mourning, and gazed upon the rugged face of the old veteran, now stiff and cold in death ; and more than one eye dropped a tear at the remembrance of the cheery smile, and the joke — sometimes superannuated, generally feeble, but always good-natured — with which the captain had been wont to greet his acquaintances. There was a growing sentiment of anger among these stern men, toward the murderer who had thus cut down their friend, and a strong feeling that ordinary justice was too slight a punishment for such a crime.

Toward noon there was an informal gathering of citizens in Dan Tyson's store.

"I hear it 'lowed that Square Kyahtah's too sick ter hol' co'te this evenin'," said one, "an' that the purlim'nary hearin' 'll haf ter go over 'tel nex' week."

A look of disappointment went round the crowd.

"Hit 's the durndes', meanes' murder ever committed in this caounty," said another, with moody emphasis.

"I s'pose the nigger 'lowed the Cap'n had some greenbacks," observed a third speaker.

"The Cap'n," said another, with an air of superior information, "has left two bairls of Confedrit money, which he 'spected 'ud be good some day er nuther."

This statement gave rise to a discussion of the speculative value of Confederate money; but in a little while the conversation returned to the murder.

"Hangin' air too good fer the murderer," said one; "he oughter be burnt, stidier bein' hung."

There was an impressive pause at this point, during which a jug of moonlight whiskey went the round of the crowd.

" Well," said a round-shouldered farmer, who, in spite of his peaceable expression and faded gray eye, was known to have been one of the most daring followers of a rebel guerrilla chieftain, " what air yer gwine ter do about it? Ef you fellers air gwine ter set down an' let a wuthless nigger kill the bes' white man in Branson, an' not say nuthin' ner do nuthin', *I'll* move outen the caounty."

This speech gave tone and direction to the rest of the conversation. Whether the fear of losing the round-shouldered farmer operated to bring about the result or not is immaterial to this narrative; but, at all events, the crowd decided to lynch the negro. They agreed that this was the least that could be done to avenge the death of their murdered friend, and that it was a becoming way in which to honor his memory. They had some vague notions of the majesty of the law and the rights of the citizen, but in the passion of the moment these sunk into oblivion; a white man had been killed by a negro.

" The Cap'n was an ole sodger," said one

of his friends solemnly. " He 'll sleep better
when he knows that a co'te-martial has be'n
hilt an' jestice done."

By agreement the lynchers were to meet at
Tyson's store at five o'clock in the afternoon,
and proceed thence to the jail, which was
situated down the Lumberton Dirt Road (as
the old turnpike antedating the plank-road
was called), about half a mile south of the
court-house. When the preliminaries of the
lynching had been arranged, and a committee
appointed to manage the affair, the crowd
dispersed, some to go to their dinners, and
some to secure recruits for the lynching party.

It was twenty minutes to five o'clock, when
an excited negro, panting and perspiring,
rushed up to the back door of Sheriff Campbell's dwelling, which stood at a little distance
from the jail and somewhat farther than the
latter building from the court-house. A tur-
baned colored woman came to the door in response to the negro's knock.

" Hoddy, Sis' Nance."

" Hoddy, Brer Sam."

" Is de shurff in," inquired the negro.

" Yas, Brer Sam, he 's eatin' his dinner,"
was the answer.

" Will yer ax 'im ter step ter de do' a minute, Sis' Nance ? "

The woman went into the dining-room, and a moment later the sheriff came to the door. He was a tall, muscular man, of a ruddier complexion than is usual among Southerners. A pair of keen, deep-set gray eyes looked out from under bushy eyebrows, and about his mouth was a masterful expression, which a full beard, once sandy in color, but now profusely sprinkled with gray, could not entirely conceal. The day was hot ; the sheriff had discarded his coat and vest, and had his white shirt open at the throat.

" What do you want, Sam ? " he inquired of the negro, who stood hat in hand, wiping the moisture from his face with a ragged shirt-sleeve.

" Shurff, dey gwine ter hang de pris'ner w'at 's lock' up in de jail. Dey 're comin' dis a-way now. I wuz layin' down on a sack er corn down at de sto', behine a pile er flour-bairls, w'en I hearn Doc' Cain en Kunnel Wright talkin' erbout it. I slip' outen de back do', en run here as fas' as I could. I hearn you say down ter de sto' once't dat you would n't let nobody take a pris'ner 'way

fum you widout walkin' over yo' dead body,
en I thought I 'd let you know 'fo' dey come,
so yer could pertec' de pris'ner."

The sheriff listened calmly, but his face grew
firmer, and a determined gleam lit up his
gray eyes. His frame grew more erect, and
he unconsciously assumed the attitude of a
soldier who momentarily expects to meet the
enemy face to face.

"Much obliged, Sam," he answered. "I 'll
protect the prisoner. Who 's coming?"

"I dunno who-all *is* comin'," replied
the negro. "Dere 's Mistah McSwayne, en
Doc' Cain, en Maje' McDonal', en Kunnel
Wright, en a heap er yuthers. I wuz so
skeered I done furgot mo' d'n half un em. I
spec' dey mus' be mos' here by dis time, so
I 'll git outen de way, fer I don' want nobody fer ter think I wuz mix' up in dis business." The negro glanced nervously down
the road toward the town, and made a movement as if to go away.

"Won't you have some dinner first?"
asked the sheriff.

The negro looked longingly in at the open
door, and sniffed the appetizing odor of boiled
pork and collards.

"I ain't got no time fer ter tarry, Shurff," he said, "but Sis' Nance mought gin me sump'n I could kyar in my han' en eat on de way."

A moment later Nancy brought him a huge sandwich of split corn-pone, with a thick slice of fat bacon inserted between the halves, and a couple of baked yams. The negro hastily replaced his ragged hat on his head, dropped the yams in the pocket of his capacious trousers, and, taking the sandwich in his hand, hurried across the road and disappeared in the woods beyond.

The sheriff reëntered the house, and put on his coat and hat. He then took down a double-barreled shotgun and loaded it with buckshot. Filling the chambers of a revolver with fresh cartridges, he slipped it into the pocket of the sack-coat which he wore.

A comely young woman in a calico dress watched these proceedings with anxious surprise.

"Where are you going, father?" she asked. She had not heard the conversation with the negro.

"I am goin' over to the jail," responded the sheriff. "There's a mob comin' this way

to lynch the nigger we 've got locked up.
But they won't do it," he added, with emphasis.

" Oh, father! don't go!'" pleaded the girl,
clinging to his arm; " they'll shoot you if you
don't give him up."

" You never mind me, Polly," said her
father reassuringly, as he gently unclasped
her hands from his arm. " I 'll take care of
myself and the prisoner, too. There ain't a
man in Branson County that would shoot me.
Besides, I have faced fire too often to be
scared away from my duty. You keep close
in the house," he continued, " and if any one
disturbs you just use the old horse-pistol in the
top bureau drawer. It 's a little old-fashioned,
but it did good work a few years ago."

The young girl shuddered at this sanguin-
ary allusion, but made no further objection to
her father's departure.

The sheriff of Branson was a man far
above the average of the community in
wealth, education, and social position. His
had been one of the few families in the
county that before the war had owned large
estates and numerous slaves. He had graduated at the State University at Chapel Hill,

and had kept up some acquaintance with current literature and advanced thought. He
had traveled some in his youth, and was
looked up to in the county as an authority on
all subjects connected with the outer world.
At first an ardent supporter of the Union, he
had opposed the secession movement in his
native State as long as opposition availed to
stem the tide of public opinion. Yielding at
last to the force of circumstances, he had entered the Confederate service rather late in
the war, and served with distinction through
several campaigns, rising in time to the rank
of colonel. After the war he had taken the
oath of allegiance, and had been chosen by
the people as the most available candidate for
the office of sheriff, to which he had been
elected without opposition. He had filled the
office for several terms, and was universally
popular with his constituents.

Colonel or Sheriff Campbell, as he was in-
differently called, as the military or civil title
happened to be most important in the opinion of the person addressing him, had a high
sense of the responsibility attaching to his
office. He had sworn to do his duty faithfully, and he knew what his duty was, as

sheriff, perhaps more clearly than he had apprehended it in other passages of his life. It was, therefore, with no uncertainty in regard to his course that he prepared his weapons and went over to the jail. He had no fears for Polly's safety.

The sheriff had just locked the heavy front door of the jail behind him when a half dozen horsemen, followed by a crowd of men on foot, came round a bend in the road and drew near the jail. They halted in front of the picket fence that surrounded the building, while several of the committee of arrangements rode on a few rods farther to the sheriff's house. One of them dismounted and rapped on the door with his riding-whip.

" Is the sheriff at home ? " he inquired.

" No, he has just gone out," replied Polly, who had come to the door.

" We want the jail keys," he continued.

" They are not here," said Polly. " The sheriff has them himself." Then she added, with assumed indifference, " He is at the jail now."

The man turned away, and Polly went into the front room, from which she peered anxiously between the slats of the green blinds

of a window that looked toward the jail.
Meanwhile the messenger returned to his
companions and announced his discovery. It
looked as though the sheriff had learned of
their design and was preparing to resist it.

One of them stepped forward and rapped
on the jail door.

" Well, what is it ? " said the sheriff, from
within.

" We want to talk to you, Sheriff," replied
the spokesman.

There was a little wicket in the door; this
the sheriff opened, and answered through it.

" All right, boys, talk away. You are all
strangers to me, and I don't know what business you can have." The sheriff did not
think it necessary to recognize anybody in
particular on such an occasion ; the question
of identity sometimes comes up in the inves-
tigation of these extra-judicial executions.

" We're a committee of citizens and we
want to get into the jail."

" What for ? It ain't much trouble to get
into jail. Most people want to keep out."

The mob was in no humor to appreciate
a joke, and the sheriff's witticism fell dead
upon an unresponsive audience.

" We want to have a talk with the nigger that killed Cap'n Walker."

" You can talk to that nigger in the court-house, when he's brought out for trial. Court will be in session here next week. I know what you fellows want, but you can't get my prisoner to-day. Do you want to take the bread out of a poor man's mouth? I get seventy-five cents a day for keeping this prisoner, and he's the only one in jail. I can't have my family suffer just to please you fellows."

One or two young men in the crowd laughed at the idea of Sheriff Campbell's suffering for want of seventy-five cents a day; but they were frowned into silence by those who stood near them.

" Ef yer don't let us in," cried a voice, " we 'll bu's' the do' open."

" Bust away," answered the sheriff, raising his voice so that all could hear. " But I give you fair warning. The first man that tries it will be filled with buckshot. I'm sheriff of this county; I know my duty, and I mean to do it."

" What's the use of kicking, Sheriff?" argued one of the leaders of the mob. " The nigger is sure to hang anyhow; he richly deserves it; and we've got to do something to teach the niggers their places, or white people won't be able to live in the county."

"There's no use talking, boys," responded the sheriff. "I'm a white man outside, but in this jail I'm sheriff; and if this nigger's to be hung in this county, I propose to do the hanging. So you fellows might as well right-about-face, and march back to Troy. You've had a pleasant trip, and the exercise will be good for you. You know *me*. I've got powder and ball, and I've faced fire before now, with nothing between me and the enemy, and I don't mean to surrender this jail while I'm able to shoot." Having thus announced his determination, the sheriff closed and fastened the wicket, and looked around for the best position from which to defend the building.

The crowd drew off a little, and the leaders conversed together in low tones.

The Branson County jail was a small, two-story brick building, strongly constructed, with no attempt at architectural ornamentation. Each story was divided into two large cells by a passage running from front to rear.

"WE'LL BU'S' THE DO' OPEN"

A grated iron door gave entrance from the passage to each of the four cells. The jail seldom had many prisoners in it, and the lower windows had been boarded up. When the sheriff had closed the wicket, he ascended the steep wooden stairs to the upper floor. There was no window at the front of the upper passage, and the most available position from which to watch the movements of the crowd below was the front window of the cell occupied by the solitary prisoner.

The sheriff unlocked the door and entered the cell. The prisoner was crouched in a corner, his yellow face, blanched with terror, looking ghastly in the semi-darkness of the room. A cold perspiration had gathered on his forehead, and his teeth were chattering with affright.

" For God's sake, Sheriff," he murmured hoarsely, " don't let 'em lynch me ; I did n't kill the old man."

The sheriff glanced at the cowering wretch with a look of mingled contempt and loathing.

" Get up," he said sharply. " You will probably be hung sooner or later, but it shall not be to-day, if I can help it. I 'll unlock your fetters, and if I can't hold the jail, you 'll

have to make the best fight you can. If I 'm
shot, I 'll consider my responsibility at an
end."

There were iron fetters on the prisoner's
ankles, and handcuffs on his wrists. These
the sheriff unlocked, and they fell clanking
to the floor.

" Keep back from the window," said the
sheriff. " They might shoot if they saw you."

The sheriff drew toward the window a pine
bench which formed a part of the scanty furniture of the cell, and laid his revolver upon
it. Then he took his gun in hand, and took
his stand at the side of the window where he
could with least exposure of himself watch the
movements of the crowd below.

The lynchers had not anticipated any determined resistance. Of course they had looked
for a formal protest, and perhaps a sufficient
show of opposition to excuse the sheriff in
the eye of any stickler for legal formalities.
They had not however come prepared to fight
a battle, and no one of them seemed willing to lead an attack upon the jail. The
leaders of the party conferred together with a
good deal of animated gesticulation, which
was visible to the sheriff from his outlook,

though the distance was too great for him to hear what was said. At length one of them broke away from the group, and rode back to the main body of the lynchers, who were restlessly awaiting orders.

" Well, boys," said the messenger, " we'll have to let it go for the present. The sheriff says he'll shoot, and he's got the drop on us this time. There ain't any of us that want to follow Cap'n Walker jest yet. Besides, the sheriff is a good fellow, and we don't want to hurt 'im. But," he added, as if to reassure the crowd, which began to show signs of disappointment, " the nigger might as well say his prayers, for he ain't got long to live."

There was a murmur of dissent from the mob, and several voices insisted that an attack be made on the jail. But pacific counsels finally prevailed, and the mob sullenly withdrew.

The sheriff stood at the window until they had disappeared around the bend in the road. He did not relax his watchfulness when the last one was out of sight. Their withdrawal might be a mere feint, to be followed by a further attempt. So closely, indeed, was his attention drawn to the outside, that he neither saw nor heard the prisoner creep stealthily across the floor, reach out his hand and secure the revolver which lay on the bench behind the sheriff, and creep as noiselessly back to his place in the corner of the room.

A moment after the last of the lynching party had disappeared there was a shot fired from the woods across the road; a bullet whistled by the window and buried itself in the wooden casing a few inches from where the sheriff was standing.   Quick as thought, with the instinct born of a semi-guerrilla army experience, he raised his gun and fired twice at the point from which a faint puff of smoke showed the hostile bullet to have been sent. He stood a moment watching, and then rested his gun against the window, and reached behind him mechanically for the other weapon. It was not on the bench.   As the sheriff realized this fact, he turned his head and looked into the muzzle of the revolver.

" Stay where you are, Sheriff," said the prisoner, his eyes glistening, his face almost ruddy with excitement.

The sheriff mentally cursed his own carelessness for allowing him to be caught in such a predicament.   He had not expected anything of the kind. He had relied on the negro's cowardice and subordination in the presence of an armed white man as a matter of course. The sheriff was a brave man, but realized that the prisoner had him at an immense disadvantage. [The two men stood thus for a moment, fighting a harmless duel with their eyes.]

"Well, what do you mean to do?" asked the sheriff with apparent calmness.

"To get away, of course," said the prisoner, in a tone which caused the sheriff to look at him more closely, and with an involuntary feeling of apprehension; if the man was not mad, he was in a state of mind akin to madness, and quite as dangerous. The sheriff felt that he must speak the prisoner fair, and watch for a chance to turn the tables on him. The keen-eyed, desperate man before him was a different being altogether from the groveling wretch who had begged so piteously for life a few minutes before.

At length the sheriff spoke : —

"Is this your gratitude to me for saving your life at the risk of my own? If I had not done so, you would now be swinging from the limb of some neighboring tree."

"True," said the prisoner, "you saved my

life, but for how long? When you came in, you said Court would sit next week. When the crowd went away they said I had not long to live. It is merely a choice of two ropes."

"While there's life there's hope," replied the sheriff. He uttered this commonplace mechanically, while his brain was busy in trying to think out some way of escape. "If you are innocent you can prove it."

The mulatto kept his eye upon the sheriff. "I didn't kill the old man," he replied; "but I shall never be able to clear myself. I was at his house at nine o'clock. I stole from it the coat that was on my back when I was taken. I would be convicted, even with a fair trial, unless the real murderer were discovered beforehand."

The sheriff knew this only too well. While he was thinking what argument next to use, the prisoner continued: —

"Throw me the keys — no, unlock the door."

The sheriff stood a moment irresolute. The mulatto's eye glittered ominously. The sheriff crossed the room and unlocked the door leading into the passage.

"Now go down and unlock the outside door."

The heart of the sheriff leaped within him. Perhaps he might make a dash for liberty, and gain the outside. He descended the narrow stairs, the prisoner keeping close behind him.

The sheriff inserted the huge iron key into the lock. The rusty bolt yielded slowly. It still remained for him to pull the door open.

"Stop!" thundered the mulatto, who seemed to divine the sheriff's purpose. "Move a muscle, and I'll blow your brains out."

The sheriff obeyed; he realized that his chance had not yet come.

"Now keep on that side of the passage, and go back upstairs."

Keeping the sheriff under cover of the revolver, the mulatto followed him up the stairs. The sheriff expected the prisoner to lock him into the cell and make his own escape. He had about come to the conclusion that the best thing he could do under the circumstances was to submit quietly, and take his chances of recapturing the prisoner after the alarm had been given. The sheriff had faced death more than once upon the battlefield. A few minutes before, well armed, and with a brick wall between him and them he had dared a hundred men to fight; but he felt instinctively that the desperate man confronting him was not to be trifled with, and he was too prudent a man to risk his life against such heavy odds. He had Polly to look after, and there was a limit beyond which devotion to duty would be quixotic and even foolish.

"I want to get away," said the prisoner, "and I don't want to be captured; for if I am I know I will be hung on the spot. I am afraid," he added somewhat reflectively, "that in order to save myself I shall have to kill you."

"Good God!" exclaimed the sheriff in involuntary terror; "you would not kill the man to whom you owe your own life."

"You speak more truly than you know," replied the mulatto. "I indeed owe my life to you."

The sheriff started. He was capable of surprise, even in that moment of extreme peril. "Who are you?" he asked in amazement.

"Tom, Cicely's son," returned the other. He had closed the door and stood talking to the sheriff through the grated opening. "Don't you remember Cicely — Cicely whom

you sold, with her child, to the speculator on
his way to Alabama?"

The sheriff did remember. He had been
sorry for it many a time since. It had been
the old story of debts, mortgages, and bad
crops. He had quarreled with the mother.
The price offered for her and her child had
been unusually large, and he had yielded
to the combination of anger and pecuniary
stress.

"Good God!" he gasped, "you would
not murder your own father?"

"My father?" replied the mulatto. "It
were well enough for me to claim the relationship, but it comes with poor grace from you
to ask anything by reason of it. What
father's duty have you ever performed for
me? Did you give me your name, or even
your protection? Other white men gave their
colored sons freedom and money, and sent
them to the free States. *You* sold *me* to the
rice swamps."

"I at least gave you the life you cling to,"
murmured the sheriff.

"Life?" said the prisoner, with a sarcastic
laugh. "What kind of a life? You gave
me your own blood, your own features, — no

man need look at us together twice to see
that, — and you gave me a black mother.
Poor wretch! She died under the lash, because she had enough womanhood to call her
soul her own. You gave me a white man's
spirit, and you made me a slave, and crushed
it out."

"But you are free now," said the sheriff.
He had not doubted, could not doubt, the
mulatto's word. He knew whose passions
coursed beneath that swarthy skin and burned
in the black eyes opposite his own. He saw
in this mulatto what he himself might have
become had not the safeguards of parental
restraint and public opinion been thrown
around him.

"Free to do what?" replied the mulatto.
"Free in name, but despised and scorned and
set aside by the people to whose race I belong
far more than to my mother's."

"There are schools," said the sheriff. "You
have been to school." He had noticed that
the mulatto spoke more eloquently and used
better language than most Branson County
people.

"I have been to school, and dreamed when
I went that it would work some marvelous

change in my condition. But what did I
learn? I learned to feel that no degree of
learning or wisdom will change the color of
my skin and that I shall always wear what in
my own country is a badge of degradation.
When I think about it seriously I do not care
particularly for such a life. It is the animal
in me, not the man, that flees the gallows.
I owe you nothing," he went on, " and expect
nothing of you; and it would be no more
than justice if I should avenge upon you my
mother's wrongs and my own. But still I
hate to shoot you; I have never yet taken
human life — for I did *not* kill the old captain. Will you promise to give no alarm and
make no attempt to capture me until morning, if I do not shoot?"

So absorbed were the two men in their col-
loquy and their own tumultuous thoughts
that neither of them had heard the door below
move upon its hinges. Neither of them had
heard a light step come stealthily up the stairs,
nor seen a slender form creep along the darkening passage toward the mulatto.

The sheriff hesitated. The struggle between his love of life and his sense of duty
was a terrific one. It may seem strange that

a man who could sell his own child into slavery should hesitate at such a moment, when his life was trembling in the balance. But the baleful influence of human slavery poisoned the very fountains of life, and created new standards of right. [The sheriff was conscientious; his conscience had merely been warped by his environment] Let no one ask what his answer would have been; he was spared the necessity of a decision.

"Stop," said the mulatto, "you need not promise. I could not trust you if you did. It is your life for mine; there is but one safe way for me; you must die."

He raised his arm to fire, when there was a flash — a report from the passage behind him. His arm fell heavily at his side, and the pistol dropped at his feet.

The sheriff recovered first from his surprise, and throwing open the door secured the fallen weapon. Then seizing the prisoner he thrust him into the cell and locked the door upon him; after which he turned to Polly, who leaned half-fainting against the wall, her hands clasped over her heart.

"Oh, father, I was just in time!" she cried hysterically, and, wildly sobbing, threw herself into her father's arms.

"I watched until they all went away," she
said. "I heard the shot from the woods and
I saw you shoot. Then when you did not
come out I feared something had happened,
that perhaps you had been wounded. I got
out the other pistol and ran over here. When
I found the door open, I knew something was
wrong, and when I heard voices I crept upstairs, and reached the top just in time to
hear him say he would kill you. Oh, it was
a narrow escape!"

When she had grown somewhat calmer, the
sheriff left her standing there and went back
into the cell. The prisoner's arm was bleeding from a flesh wound. His bravado had
given place to a stony apathy. There was
no sign in his face of fear or disappointment
or feeling of any kind. The sheriff sent
Polly to the house for cloth, and bound up
the prisoner's wound with a rude skill acquired during his army life.

"I'll have a doctor come and dress the
wound in the morning," he said to the prisoner. "It will do very well until then, if
you will keep quiet. If the doctor asks you
how the wound was caused, you can say that
you were struck by the bullet fired from the

woods. It would do you no good to have it
known that you were shot while attempting
to escape."

The prisoner uttered no word of thanks or
apology, but sat in sullen silence. When the
wounded arm had been bandaged, Polly and
her father returned to the house.

The sheriff was in an unusually thoughtful
mood that evening. He put salt in his coffee
at supper, and poured vinegar over his pan-
cakes. To many of Polly's questions he returned random answers. When he had gone
to bed he lay awake for several hours.

In the silent watches of the night, when he
was alone with God, there came into his mind
a flood of unaccustomed thoughts. An hour
or two before, standing face to face with
death, he had experienced a sensation similar
to that which drowning men are said to feel
— a kind of clarifying of the moral faculty,
in which the veil of the flesh, with its obscur-
ing passions and prejudices, is pushed aside
for a moment, and all the acts of one's life
stand out, in the clear light of truth, in their
correct proportions and relations, — a state of
mind in which one sees himself as God may
be supposed to see him. In the reaction

following his rescue, this feeling had given
place for a time to far different emotions.
But now, in the silence of midnight, something of this clearness of spirit returned to
the sheriff. [He saw that he had owed some
duty to this son of his,— that neither law nor
custom could destroy a responsibility inherent
in the nature of mankind.] He could not
thus, in the eyes of God at least, shake off the
consequences of his sin. Had he never sinned,
this wayward spirit would never have come
back from the vanished past to haunt him.
As these thoughts came, his anger against
the mulatto died away, and in its place there
sprang up a great pity. The hand of parental authority might have restrained the passions he had seen burning in the prisoner's
eyes when the desperate man spoke the words
which had seemed to doom his father to death.
The sheriff felt that he might have saved this
fiery spirit from the slough of slavery; that
he might have sent him to the free North,
and given him there, or in some other land,
an opportunity to turn to usefulness and honorable pursuits the talents that had run to crime,
perhaps to madness ; he might, still less, have
given this son of his the poor simulacrum of

liberty which men of his caste could possess in a slave-holding community ; or least of all, but still something, he might have kept the boy on the plantation, where the burdens of slavery would have fallen lightly upon him.

The sheriff recalled his own youth. He had inherited an honored name to keep untarnished ; he had had a future to make ; the picture of a fair young bride had beckoned him on to happiness. The poor wretch now stretched upon a pallet of straw between the brick walls of the jail had had none of these things, — no name, no father, no mother — in the true meaning of motherhood, — and until the past few years no possible future, and then one vague and shadowy in its outline, and dependent for form and substance upon the slow solution of a problem in which there were many unknown quantities.

From what he might have done to what he might yet do was an easy transition for the awakened conscience of the sheriff. It occurred to him, purely as a hypothesis, that he might permit his prisoner to escape ; but his oath of office, his duty as sheriff, stood in the way of such a course, and the sheriff dismissed the idea from his mind. He could, however, investigate the circumstances of the

murder, and move Heaven and earth to discover
the real criminal, for he no longer doubted the
prisoner's innocence ; he could employ counsel
for the accused, and perhaps influence public
opinion in his favor.   An acquittal once
secured, some plan could be devised by which
the sheriff might in some degree atone for his
crime against this son of his — against society
— against God.

When the sheriff had reached this conclusion he fell into an unquiet slumber, from
which he awoke late the next morning.

He went over to the jail before breakfast
and found the prisoner lying on his pallet,
his face turned to the wall ; he did not move
when the sheriff rattled the door.

" Good-morning," said the latter, in a tone
intended to waken the prisoner.

There was no response.   The sheriff looked
more keenly at the recumbent figure ; there
was an unnatural rigidity about its attitude.

He hastily unlocked the door and, entering
the cell, bent over the prostrate form.   There
was no sound of breathing ; he turned the
body over — it was cold and stiff.   The prisoner had torn the bandage from his wound
and bled to death during the night.   He had
evidently been dead several hours.

A MATTER OF PRINCIPLE

I

"WHAT our country needs most in its treatment of the race problem," observed Mr. Cicero Clayton at one of the monthly meetings of the Blue Vein Society, of which he was a prominent member, "is a clearer conception of the brotherhood of man."

The same sentiment in much the same words had often fallen from Mr. Clayton's lips, — so often, in fact, that the younger members of the society sometimes spoke of him — among themselves of course — as "Brotherhood Clayton." The sobriquet derived its point from the application he made of the principle involved in this oft-repeated proposition.

The fundamental article of Mr. Clayton's social creed was that he himself was not a negro.

"I know," he would say, "that the white people lump us all together as negroes, and

condemn us all to the same social ostracism.
But I don't accept this classification, for my
part, and I imagine that, as the chief party
in interest, I have a right to my opinion.
People who belong by half or more of their
blood to the most virile and progressive race
of modern times have as much right to call
themselves white as others have to call them
negroes."

Mr. Clayton spoke warmly, for he was well
informed, and had thought much upon the
subject; too much, indeed, for he had not
been able to escape entirely the tendency of
too much concentration upon one subject to
make even the clearest minds morbid.

"Of course we can't enforce our claims, or
protect ourselves from being robbed of our
birthright; but we can at least have principles, and try to live up to them the best we
can. If we are not accepted as white, we can
at any rate make it clear that we object to
being called black. Our protest cannot fail
in time to impress itself upon the better class
of white people; for the Anglo-Saxon race
loves justice, and will eventually do it, where
it does not conflict with their own interests."

Whether or not the fact that Mr. Clayton

meant no sarcasm, and was conscious of no
inconsistency in this eulogy, tended to establish the racial identity he claimed may safely
be left to the discerning reader.

In living up to his creed Mr. Clayton declined to associate to any considerable extent
with black people. This was sometimes a
little inconvenient, and occasionally involved
a sacrifice of some pleasure for himself and
his family, because they would not attend entertainments where many black people were
likely to be present. But they had a social
refuge in a little society of people like themselves; they attended, too, a church, of which
nearly all the members were white, and they
were connected with a number of the religious
and benevolent associations open to all good
citizens, where they came into contact with
the better class of white people, and were
treated, in their capacity of members, with
a courtesy and consideration scarcely different from that accorded to other citizens.

Mr. Clayton's racial theory was not only
logical enough, but was in his own case backed
up by substantial arguments. He had begun
life with a small patrimony, and had invested
his money in a restaurant, which by careful

and judicious attention had grown from a cheap eating-house into the most popular and successful confectionery and catering establishment in Groveland. His business occupied a double store on Oakwood Avenue. He owned houses and lots, and stocks and bonds, had good credit at the banks, and lived in a style befitting his income and business standing. In person he was of olive complexion, with slightly curly hair. His features approached the Cuban or Latin-American type rather than the familiar broad characteristics of the mulatto, this suggestion of something foreign being heightened by a Vandyke beard and a carefully waxed and pointed mustache. When he walked to church on Sunday mornings with his daughter Alice, they were a couple of such striking appearance as surely to attract attention.

Miss Alice Clayton was queen of her social set. She was young, she was handsome. She was nearly white; she frankly confessed her sorrow that she was not entirely so. She was accomplished and amiable, dressed in good taste, and had for her father by all odds the richest colored man — the term is used with apologies to Mr. Clayton, explaining that it

does not necessarily mean a negro — in Groveland. So pronounced was her superiority that
really she had but one social rival worthy of
the name, — Miss Lura Watkins, whose father kept a prosperous livery stable and lived
in almost as good style as the Claytons. Miss
Watkins, while good-looking enough, was not
so young nor quite so white as Miss Clayton.
She was popular, however, among their mutual acquaintances, and there was a good-
natured race between the two as to which
should make the first and best marriage.

Marriages among Miss Clayton's set were
serious affairs.   Of course marriage is always
a serious matter, whether it be a success or a
failure, and there are those who believe that
any marriage is better than no marriage.   But
among Miss Clayton's friends and associates
matrimony took on an added seriousness because of the very narrow limits within which
it could take place.   Miss Clayton and her
friends, by reason of their assumed superiority
to black people, or perhaps as much by reason of a somewhat morbid shrinking from the
curiosity manifested toward married people of
strongly contrasting colors, would not marry
black men, and except in rare instances white

men would not marry them. They were
therefore restricted for a choice to the young
men of their own complexion. But these,
unfortunately for the girls, had a wider choice.
In any State where the laws permit freedom
of the marriage contract, a man, by virtue of
his sex, can find a wife of whatever complexion
he prefers; of course he must not always ask
too much in other respects, for most women
like to better their social position when they
marry. To the number thus lost by " going
on the other side," as the phrase went, add
the worthless contingent whom no self-respect-
ing woman would marry, and the choice was
still further restricted; so that it had become
fashionable, when the supply of eligible men
ran short, for those of Miss Clayton's set who
could afford it to go traveling, ostensibly for
pleasure, but with the serious hope that they
might meet their fate away from home.

Miss Clayton had perhaps a larger option
than any of her associates. Among such men
as there were she could have taken her choice.
Her beauty, her position, her accomplishments,
her father's wealth, all made her eminently
desirable. But, on the other hand, the same
things rendered her more difficult to reach, and

harder to please. To get access to her heart, too, it was necessary to run the gauntlet of her parents, which, until she had reached the age of twenty-three, no one had succeeded in doing safely. Many had called, but none had been chosen.

There was, however, one spot left unguarded, and through it Cupid, a veteran sharpshooter, sent a dart. Mr. Clayton had taken into his service and into his household a poor relation, a sort of cousin several times removed. This boy — his name was Jack — had gone into Mr. Clayton's service at a very youthful age, — twelve or thirteen. He had helped about the housework, washed the dishes, swept the floors, taken care of the lawn and the stable for three or four years, while he attended school. His cousin had then taken him into the store, where he had swept the floor, washed the windows, and done a class of work that kept fully impressed upon him the fact that he was a poor dependent. Nevertheless he was a cheerful lad, who took what he could get and was properly grateful, but always meant to get more. By sheer force of industry and affability and shrewdness, he forced his employer to promote him in time

to a position of recognized authority in the
establishment. Any one outside of the family
would have perceived in him a very suitable
husband for Miss Clayton ; he was of about
the same age, or a year or two older, was as
fair of complexion as she, when she was not
powdered, and was passably good-looking,
with a bearing of which the natural manli-
ness had been no more warped than his training and racial status had rendered inevitable ;
for he had early learned the law of growth,
that to bend is better than to break. He
was sometimes sent to accompany Miss Clayton to places in the evening, when she had no
other escort, and it is quite likely that she
discovered his good points before her parents
did. That they should in time perceive them
was inevitable. But even then, so accustomed
were they to looking down upon the object of
their former bounty, that they only spoke of
the matter jocularly.

"Well, Alice," her father would say in his
bluff way, "you 'll not be absolutely obliged
to die an old maid. If we can't find anything
better for you, there 's always Jack. As long
as he does n't take to some other girl, you can
fall back on him as a last chance. He 'd be
glad to take you to get into the business."

Miss Alice had considered the joke a very poor one when first made, but by occasional repetition she became somewhat familiar with it. In time it got around to Jack himself, to whom it seemed no joke at all. He had long considered it a consummation devoutly to be wished, and when he became aware that the possibility of such a match had occurred to the other parties in interest, he made up his mind that the idea should in due course of time become an accomplished fact. He had even suggested as much to Alice, in a casual way, to feel his ground; and while she had treated the matter lightly, he was not without hope that she had been impressed by the suggestion. Before he had had time, however, to follow up this lead, Miss Clayton, in the spring of 187–, went away on a visit to Washington.

The occasion of her visit was a presidential inauguration. The new President owed his nomination mainly to the votes of the Southern delegates in the convention, and was believed to be correspondingly well disposed to the race from which the Southern delegates were for the most part recruited. Friends of rival and unsuccessful candidates for the nomination had more than hinted that the

Southern delegates were very substantially
rewarded for their support at the time when
it was given; whether this was true or not
the parties concerned know best. At any rate
the colored politicians did not see it in that
light, for they were gathered from near and
far to press their claims for recognition and
patronage. On the evening following the
White House inaugural ball, the colored people of Washington gave an "inaugural" ball
at a large public hall. It was under the man-
agement of their leading citizens, among them
several high officials holding over from the last
administration, and a number of professional
and business men. This ball was the most
noteworthy social event that colored circles up
to that time had ever known. There were
many visitors from various parts of the country. Miss Clayton attended the ball, the
honors of which she carried away easily. She
danced with several partners, and was introduced to innumerable people whom she had
never seen before, and whom she hardly expected ever to meet again. She went away
from the ball, at four o'clock in the morning,
in a glow of triumph, and with a confused
impression of senators and representatives and

lawyers and doctors of all shades, who had
sought an introduction, led her through the
dance, and overwhelmed her with compliments.
She returned home the next day but one, after
the most delightful week of her life.

II

One afternoon, about three weeks after
her return from Washington, Alice received
a letter through the mail. The envelope
bore the words " House of Representatives "
printed in one corner, and in the opposite
corner, in a bold running hand, a Congressman's frank, " Hamilton M. Brown,
M. C. " The letter read as follows : —

HOUSE OF REPRESENTATIVES,
WASHINGTON, D. C., March 30, 187-.
MISS ALICE CLAYTON, GROVELAND.

DEAR FRIEND (if I may be permitted to call
you so after so brief an acquaintance), — I
remember with sincerest pleasure our recent
meeting at the inaugural ball, and the sensation created by your beauty, your amiable
manners, and your graceful dancing. Time
has so strengthened the impression I then
received, that I should have felt inconsolable

had I thought it impossible ever to again behold the charms which had brightened the occasion of our meeting and eclipsed by their brilliancy the leading belles of the capital. I had hoped, however, to have the pleasure of meeting you again, and circumstances have fortunately placed it in my power to do so at an early date. You have doubtless learned that the contest over the election in the Sixth Congressional District of South Carolina has been decided in my favor, and that I now have the honor of representing my native State at the national capital. I have just been appointed a member of a special committee to visit and inspect the Sault River and the Straits of Mackinac, with reference to the needs of lake navigation. I have made arrangements to start a week ahead of the other members of the committee, whom I am to meet in Detroit on the 20th. I shall leave here on the 2d, and will arrive in Groveland on the 3d, by the 7.30 evening express. I shall remain in Groveland several days, in the course of which I shall be pleased to call, and renew the acquaintance so auspiciously begun in Washington, which it is my fondest hope may ripen into a warmer friendship.

If you do not regard my visit as presumptuous, and do not write me in the mean while forbidding it, I shall do myself the pleasure of waiting on you the morning after my arrival in Groveland.

With renewed expressions of my sincere admiration and profound esteem, I remain,

Sincerely yours,

HAMILTON M. BROWN, M. C.

To Alice, and especially to her mother, this bold and flowery letter had very nearly the force of a formal declaration. They read it over again and again, and spent most of the afternoon discussing it. There were few young men in Groveland eligible as husbands for so superior a person as Alice Clayton, and an addition to the number would be very acceptable. But the mere fact of his being a Congressman was not sufficient to qualify him; there were other considerations.

" I've never heard of this Honorable Hamilton M. Brown," said Mr. Clayton. The letter had been laid before him at the supper-table. " It's strange, Alice, that you have n't said anything about him before. You must have met lots of swell folks not to recollect a Congressman."

" But he was n't a Congressman then," answered Alice; " he was only a claimant. I remember Senator Bruce, and Mr. Douglass; but there were so many doctors and lawyers and politicians that I could n't keep track of them all. Still I have a faint impression of a Mr. Brown who danced with me."

She went into the parlor and brought out the dancing programme she had used at the Washington ball. She had decorated it with a bow of blue ribbon and preserved it as a souvenir of her visit.

" Yes," she said, after examining it, " I must have danced with him. Here are the initials — ' H. M. B.' "

" What color is he ? " asked Mr. Clayton, as he plied his knife and fork.

" I have a notion that he was rather dark — darker than any one I had ever danced with before."

" Why did you dance with him ? " asked her father. " You were n't obliged to go back on your principles because you were away from home."

" Well, father, ' when you 're in Rome ' — you know the rest. Mrs. Clearweather introduced me to several dark men, to him among others. They were her friends, and common decency required me to be courteous."

"If this man is black, we don't want to encourage him. If he's the right sort, we'll invite him to the house."

"And make him feel at home," added Mrs. Clayton, on hospitable thoughts intent.

"We must ask Sadler about him to-morrow," said Mr. Clayton, when he had drunk his coffee and lighted his cigar. "If he's the right man he shall have cause to remember his visit to Groveland. We'll show him that Washington is not the only town on earth."

The uncertainty of the family with regard to Mr. Brown was soon removed. Mr. Solomon Sadler, who was supposed to know everything worth knowing concerning the colored race, and everybody of importance connected with it, dropped in after supper to make an evening call. Sadler was familiar with the history of every man of negro ancestry who had distinguished himself in any walk of life. He could give the pedigree of Alexander Pushkin, the titles of scores of Dumas's novels (even Sadler had not time to learn them all), and could recite the whole of Wendell

Phillips's lecture on Toussaint l'Ouverture. He claimed a personal acquaintance with Mr. Frederick Douglass, and had been often in Washington, where he was well known and well received in good colored society.

"Let me see," he said reflectively, when asked for information about the Honorable Hamilton M. Brown. "Yes, I think I know him. He studied at Oberlin just after the war. He was about leaving there when I entered. There were two H. M. Browns there — a Hamilton M. Brown and a Henry M. Brown. One was stout and dark and the other was slim and quite light; you could scarcely tell him from a dark white man. They used to call them 'light Brown' and 'dark Brown.' I did n't know either of them except by sight, for they were there only a few weeks after I went in. As I remember them, Hamilton was the fair one — a very good-looking, gentlemanly fellow, and, as I heard, a good student and a fine speaker."

"Do you remember what kind of hair he had?" asked Mr. Clayton.

"Very good indeed; straight, as I remember it. He looked something like a Spaniard or a Portuguese."

"Now that you describe him," said Alice, "I remember quite well dancing with such a gentleman; and I'm wrong about my 'H. M. B.' The dark man must have been some one else; there are two others on my card that I can't remember distinctly, and he was probably one of those."

"I guess he's all right, Alice," said her father when Sadler had gone away. "He evidently means business, and we must treat him white. Of course he must stay with us; there are no hotels in Groveland while he is here. Let's see — he'll be here in three days. That is n't very long, but I guess we can get ready. I'll write a letter this afternoon — or you write it, and invite him to the house, and say I'll meet him at the depot. And you may have *carte blanche* for making the preparations."

"We must have some people to meet him."

"Certainly; a reception is the proper thing. Sit down immediately and write the letter and I'll mail it first thing in the morning, so he'll get it before he has time to make other arrangements. And you and your mother put your heads together and make out a list of guests, and I'll have the invitations printed to-morrow. We will show the darkeys of Groveland how to entertain a Congressman."

It will be noted that in moments of abstraction or excitement Mr. Clayton sometimes relapsed into forms of speech not entirely consistent with his principles. But some allowance must be made for his atmosphere; he could no more escape from it than the leopard can change his spots, or the — In deference to Mr. Clayton's feelings the quotation will be left incomplete.

Alice wrote the letter on the spot and it was duly mailed, and sped on its winged way to Washington.

The preparations for the reception were made as thoroughly and elaborately as possible on so short a notice. The invitations were issued; the house was cleaned from attic to cellar; an orchestra was engaged for the evening; elaborate floral decorations were planned and the flowers ordered. Even the refreshments, which ordinarily, in the household of a caterer, would be mere matter of familiar detail, became a subject of serious consultation and study.

The approaching event was a matter of

very much interest to the fortunate ones who
were honored with invitations, and this for
several reasons. They were anxious to meet
this sole representative of their race in the
—th Congress, and as he was not one of the
old-line colored leaders, but a new star risen
on the political horizon, there was a special
curiosity to see who he was and what he
looked like. Moreover, the Claytons did not
often entertain a large company, but when
they did, it was on a scale commensurate with
their means and position, and to be present
on such an occasion was a thing to remember
and to talk about. And, most important
consideration of all, some remarks dropped
by members of the Clayton family had given
rise to the rumor that the Congressman was
seeking a wife. This invested his visit with
a romantic interest, and gave the reception a
practical value; for there were other marriage-
able girls besides Miss Clayton, and if one
was left another might be taken.

III

On the evening of April 3d, at fifteen
minutes of six o'clock, Mr. Clayton, accom-

panied by Jack, entered the livery carriage
waiting at his gate and ordered the coachman
to drive to the Union Depot. He had taken
Jack along, partly for company, and partly
that Jack might relieve the Congressman of
any trouble about his baggage, and make
himself useful in case of emergency. Jack
was willing enough to go, for he had foreseen
in the visitor a rival for Alice's hand, — indeed he had heard more or less of the subject
for several days, — and was glad to make a
reconnaissance before the enemy arrived upon
the field of battle. He had made — at least
he had thought so — considerable progress
with Alice during the three weeks since her
return from Washington, and once or twice
Alice had been perilously near the tender
stage. This visit had disturbed the situation
and threatened to ruin his chances; but he
did not mean to give up without a struggle.

Arrived at the main entrance, Mr. Clayton
directed the carriage to wait, and entered the
station with Jack. The Union Depot at
Groveland was an immense oblong structure,
covering a dozen parallel tracks and furnishing
terminal passenger facilities for half a dozen
railroads. The tracks ran east and west, and

the depot was entered from the south, at
about the middle of the building.   On either
side of the entrance, the waiting-rooms, re-
freshment rooms, baggage and express depart-
ments, and other administrative offices, extended in a row for the entire length of the
building ; and beyond them and parallel with
them stretched a long open space, separated
from the tracks by an iron fence or *grille*.
There were two entrance gates in the fence,
at which tickets must be shown before access
could be had to trains, and two other gates,
by which arriving passengers came out.

Mr. Clayton looked at the blackboard on
the wall underneath the station clock, and
observed that the 7.30 train from Washington was five minutes late.   Accompanied by
Jack he walked up and down the platform
until the train, with the usual accompaniment
of panting steam and clanging bell and rum-
bling trucks, pulled into the station, and drew
up on the third or fourth track from the iron
railing.   Mr. Clayton stationed himself at the
gate nearest the rear end of the train, reason-
ing that the Congressman would ride in a parlor car, and would naturally come out by the
gate nearest the point at which he left the
train.

"You'd better go and stand by the other gate, Jack," he said to his companion, "and stop him if he goes out that way."

The train was well filled and a stream of passengers poured through. Mr. Clayton scanned the crowd carefully as they approached the gate, and scrutinized each passenger as he came through, without seeing any one that met the description of Congressman Brown, as given by Sadler, or any one that could in his opinion be the gentleman for whom he was looking. When the last one had passed through he was left to the conclusion that his expected guest had gone out by the other gate. Mr. Clayton hastened thither.

"Didn't he come out this way, Jack?" he asked.

"No, sir," replied the young man, "I haven't seen him."

"That's strange," mused Mr. Clayton, somewhat anxiously. "He would hardly fail to come without giving us notice. Surely we must have missed him. We'd better look around a little. You go that way and I'll go this."

Mr. Clayton turned and walked several

rods along the platform to the men's waiting-
room, and standing near the door glanced
around to see if he could find the object of
his search.   The only colored person in the
room was a stout and very black man, wearing a broadcloth suit and a silk hat, and
seated a short distance from the door.   On
the seat by his side stood a couple of valises.
On one of them, the one nearest him, on
which his arm rested, was written, in white
letters, plainly legible, —

> " H. M. BROWN, M. C.
> " Washington, D. C."

Mr. Clayton's feelings at this discovery can
better be imagined than described. He hastily
left the waiting-room, before the black gentleman, who was looking the other way, was
even aware of his presence, and, walking
rapidly up and down the platform, communed
with himself upon what course of action the
situation demanded. He had invited to his
house, had come down to meet, had made
elaborate preparations to entertain on the following evening, a light-colored man, — a white
man by his theory, an acceptable guest, a
possible husband for his daughter, an avowed

suitor for her hand. If the Congressman had turned out to be brown, even dark brown, with fairly good hair, though he might not have desired him as a son-in-law, yet he could have welcomed him as a guest. But even this softening of the blow was denied him, for the man in the waiting-room was palpably, aggressively black, with pronounced African features and woolly hair, without apparently a single drop of redeeming white blood. Could he, in the face of his well-known principles, his lifelong rule of conduct, take this negro into his home and introduce him to his friends? Could he subject his wife and daughter to the rude shock of such a disappointment? It would be bad enough for them to learn of the ghastly mistake, but to have him in the house would be twisting the arrow in the wound.

Mr. Clayton had the instincts of a gentleman, and realized the delicacy of the situation. But to get out of his difficulty without wounding the feelings of the Congressman required not only diplomacy but dispatch. Whatever he did must be done promptly; for if he waited many minutes the Congressman would probably take a carriage and be driven to Mr. Clayton's residence.

A ray of hope came for a moment to illumine the gloom of the situation. Perhaps the black man was merely sitting there, and not the owner of the valise! For there were two valises, one on each side of the supposed Congressman. For obvious reasons he did not care to make the inquiry himself, so he looked around for his companion, who came up a moment later.

"Jack," he exclaimed excitedly, "I'm afraid we're in the worst kind of a hole, unless there's some mistake! Run down to the men's waiting-room and you'll see a man and a valise, and you'll understand what I mean. Ask that darkey if he is the Honorable Mr. Brown, Congressman from South Carolina. If he says yes, come back right away and let me know, without giving him time to ask any questions, and put your wits to work to help me out of the scrape."

"I wonder what's the matter?" said Jack to himself, but did as he was told. In a moment he came running back.

"Yes, sir," he announced; "he says he's the man."

"Jack," said Mr. Clayton desperately, "if you want to show your appreciation of what

I 've done for you, you must suggest some
way out of this. I 'd never dare to take that
negro to my house, and yet I 'm obliged to
treat him like a gentleman."

Jack's eyes had worn a somewhat reflective
look since he had gone to make the inquiry.
Suddenly his face brightened with intelligence, and then, as a newsboy ran into the
station calling his wares, hardened into determination.

" Clarion, special extry 'dition! All about
de epidemic er dipt'eria!' " clamored the newsboy with shrill childish treble, as he made his
way toward the waiting-room. Jack darted
after him, and saw the man to whom he had
spoken buy a paper. He ran back to his employer, and dragged him over toward the
ticket-seller's window.

"I have it, sir!" he exclaimed, seizing a
telegraph blank and writing rapidly, and
reading aloud as he wrote. "How 's this for
a way out?" —

" DEAR SIR, — I write you this note here
in the depot to inform you of an unfortunate
event which has interfered with my plans and
those of my family for your entertainment

while in Groveland.   Yesterday my daughter
Alice complained of a sore throat, which by
this afternoon had developed into a case of
malignant diphtheria.   In consequence our
house has been quarantined ; and while I have
felt myself obliged to come down to the
depot, I do not feel that I ought to expose
you to the possibility of infection, and I
therefore send you this by another hand.
The bearer will conduct you to a carriage
which I have ordered placed at your service,
and unless you should prefer some other
hotel, you will be driven to the Forest Hill
House, where I beg you will consider yourself
my guest during your stay in the city, and
make the fullest use of every convenience it
may offer.   From present indications I fear
no one of our family will be able to see you,
which we shall regret beyond expression, as
we have made elaborate arrangements for
your entertainment.   I still hope, however,
that you may enjoy your visit, as there are
many places of interest in the city, and many
friends will doubtless be glad to make your
acquaintance.

"With assurances of my profound regret,
I am   Sincerely yours,
"CICERO CLAYTON."

"Splendid!" cried Mr. Clayton. "You've helped me out of a horrible scrape. Now, go and take him to the hotel and see him comfortably located, and tell them to charge the bill to me."

"I suspect, sir," suggested Jack, "that I'd better not go up to the house, and you'll have to stay in yourself for a day or two, to keep up appearances. I'll sleep on the lounge at the store, and we can talk business over the telephone."

"All right, Jack, we'll arrange the details later. But for Heaven's sake get him started, or he'll be calling a hack to drive up to the house. I'll go home on a street car."

"So far so good," sighed Mr. Clayton to himself as he escaped from the station. "Jack is a deuced clever fellow, and I'll have to do something more for him. But the tug-of-war is yet to come. I've got to bribe a doctor, shut up the house for a day or two, and have all the ill-humor of two disappointed women to endure until this negro leaves town. Well, I'm sure my wife and Alice will back me up at any cost. No sacrifice is too great to escape having to entertain him; of course I have no prejudice against his color, — he

can't help that, — but it is the *principle* of
the thing.   If we received him it would be a
concession fatal to all my views and theories.
And I am really doing him a kindness, for
I'm sure that all the world could not make
Alice and her mother treat him with anything
but cold politeness.   It'll be a great mortifi-
cation to Alice, but I don't see how else I
could have got out of it."

He boarded the first car that left the depot,
and soon reached home.   The house was
lighted up, and through the lace curtains of
the parlor windows he could see his wife and
daughter, elegantly dressed, waiting to receive
their distinguished visitor.   He rang the bell
impatiently, and a servant opened the door.

"The gentleman did n't come?" asked the
maid.

"No," he said as he hung up his hat.
This brought the ladies to the door.

"He   did n't   come?"   they   exclaimed.
"What's the matter?"

"I'll tell you," he said.   "Mary," this to
the servant, a white girl, who stood in open-
eyed curiosity, "we shan't need you any more
to-night."

Then he went into the parlor, and, closing

the door, told his story. When he reached the
point where he had discovered the color of
the honorable Mr. Brown, Miss Clayton caught
her breath, and was on the verge of collapse.

"That nigger," said Mrs. Clayton indignantly, "can never set foot in this house.
But what did you do with him?"

Mr. Clayton quickly unfolded his plan, and
described the disposition he had made of the
Congressman.

"It's an awful shame," said Mrs. Clayton.
"Just think of the trouble and expense we
have gone to! And poor Alice'll never get
over it, for everybody knows he came to see
her and that he's smitten with her. But
you've done just right; we never would have
been able to hold up our heads again if we
had introduced a black man, even a Congressman, to the people that are invited here to-
morrow night, as a sweetheart of Alice.
Why, she wouldn't marry him if he was
President of the United States and plated
with gold an inch thick. The very idea!"

"Well," said Mr. Clayton, "then we've
got to act quick. Alice must wrap up her
throat — by the way, Alice, how *is* your
throat?"

"It's sore," sobbed Alice, who had been in tears almost from her father's return, "and I don't care if I do have diphtheria and die, no, I don't!" and she wept on.

"Wrap up your throat and go to bed, and I'll go over to Doctor Pillsbury's and get a diphtheria card to nail up on the house. In the morning, first thing, we'll have to write notes recalling the invitations for to-morrow evening, and have them delivered by messenger boys. We were fools for not finding out all about this man from some one who knew, before we invited him here. Sadler don't know more than half he thinks he does, anyway. And we'll have to do this thing thoroughly, or our motives will be misconstrued, and people will say we are prejudiced and all that, when it is only a matter of principle with us."

The programme outlined above was carried out to the letter. The invitations were recalled, to the great disappointment of the invited guests. The family physician called several times during the day. Alice remained in bed, and the maid left without notice, in such a hurry that she forgot to take her best clothes.

Mr. Clayton himself remained at home. He had a telephone in the house, and was therefore in easy communication with his office, so that the business did not suffer materially by reason of his absence from the store. About ten o'clock in the morning a note came up from the hotel, expressing Mr. Brown's regrets and sympathy. Toward noon Mr. Clayton picked up the morning paper, which he had not theretofore had time to read, and was glancing over it casually, when his eye fell upon a column headed "A Colored Congressman." He read the article with astonishment that rapidly turned to chagrin and dismay. It was an interview describing the Congressman as a tall and shapely man, about thirty-five years old, with an olive complexion not noticeably darker than many a white man's, straight hair, and eyes as black as sloes.

" The bearing of this son of South Carolina reveals the polished manners of the Southern gentleman, and neither from his appearance nor his conversation would one suspect that the white blood which flows in his veins in such preponderating measure had ever been crossed by that of a darker race," wrote the reporter, who had received instructions at the office that for urgent business considerations the lake shipping interest wanted Representative Brown treated with marked consideration.

There was more of the article, but the introductory portion left Mr. Clayton in such a state of bewilderment that the paper fell from his hand. What was the meaning of it? Had he been mistaken? Obviously so, or else the reporter was wrong, which was manifestly improbable. When he had recovered himself somewhat, he picked up the newspaper and began reading where he had left off.

" Representative Brown traveled to Groveland in company with Bishop Jones of the African Methodist Jerusalem Church, who is *en route* to attend the general conference of his denomination at Detroit next week. The bishop, who came in while the writer was interviewing Mr. Brown, is a splendid type of the pure negro. He is said to be a man of great power among his people, which may easily be believed after one has looked upon his expressive countenance and heard him discuss the questions which affect the welfare of his church and his race."

Mr. Clayton stared at the paper. " ' The bishop,' " he repeated, " ' is a splendid type of the pure negro. I must have mistaken the bishop for the Congressman ! But how in the world did Jack get the thing balled up ? I 'll call up the store and demand an explanation of him.

" Jack," he asked, " what kind of a looking man was the fellow you gave the note to at the depot ? "

" He was a very wicked-looking fellow, sir," came back the answer. " He had a bad eye, looked like a gambler, sir. I am not surprised that you did n't want to entertain him, even if he was a Congressman."

" What color was he — that 's what I want to know — and what kind of hair did he have ? "

" Why, he was about my complexion, sir, and had straight black hair."

The rules of the telephone company did not permit swearing over the line. Mr. Clayton broke the rules.

" Was there any one else with him ? " he asked when he had relieved his mind.

" Yes, sir, Bishop Jones of the African Methodist Jerusalem Church was sitting there with him ; they had traveled from Washington together.   I drove the bishop to his stopping-place after I had left Mr. Brown at the hotel.   I did n't suppose you 'd mind."

Mr. Clayton fell into a chair, and indulged in thoughts unutterable.

He folded up the paper and slipped it under the family Bible, where it was least likely to be soon discovered.

"I 'll hide the paper, anyway," he groaned. "I 'll never hear the last of this till my dying day, so I may as well have a few hours' respite.   It 's too late to go back, and we 've got to play the farce out.   Alice is really sick with disappointment, and to let her know this now would only make her worse.   May be he 'll leave town in a day or two, and then she 'll be in condition to stand it.   Such luck is enough to disgust a man with trying to do right and live up to his principles."

Time hung a little heavy on Mr. Clayton's hands during the day.   His wife was busy with the housework.   He answered several telephone calls about Alice's health, and called up the store occasionally to ask how the business was getting on.   After lunch he lay down on a sofa and took a nap, from which

he was aroused by the sound of the door-bell.
He went to the door. The evening paper was
lying on the porch, and the newsboy, who had
not observed the diphtheria sign until after he
had rung, was hurrying away as fast as his
legs would carry him.

Mr. Clayton opened the paper and looked
it through to see if there was any reference
to the visiting Congressman. He found what
he sought and more. An article on the local
page contained a résumé of the information
given in the morning paper, with the following additional paragraph : —

"A reporter, who called at the Forest Hill
this morning to interview Representative
Brown, was informed that the Congressman
had been invited to spend the remainder of
his time in Groveland as the guest of Mr.
William Watkins, the proprietor of the popular livery establishment on Main Street. Mr.
Brown will remain in the city several days, and
a reception will be tendered him at Mr. Watkins's on Wednesday evening."

"That ends it," sighed Mr. Clayton. "The
dove of peace will never again rest on my
roof-tree."

But why dwell longer on the sufferings of

Mr. Clayton, or attempt to describe the feelings or chronicle the remarks of his wife and daughter when they learned the facts in the case?

As to Representative Brown, he was made welcome in the hospitable home of Mr. William Watkins. There was a large and brilliant assemblage at the party on Wednesday evening, at which were displayed the costumes prepared for the Clayton reception. Mr. Brown took a fancy to Miss Lura Watkins, to whom, before the week was over, he became engaged to be married. Meantime poor Alice, the innocent victim of circumstances and principles, lay sick abed with a supposititious case of malignant diphtheria, and a real case of acute disappointment and chagrin.

"Oh, Jack!" exclaimed Alice, a few weeks later, on the way home from evening church in company with the young man, "what a dreadful thing it all was! And to think of that hateful Lura Watkins marrying the Congressman!"

The street was shaded by trees at the point where they were passing, and there was no one in sight. Jack put his arm around her waist, and, leaning over, kissed her.

"Never mind, dear," he said soothingly, "you still have your 'last chance' left, and I 'll prove myself a better man than the Congressman."

Occasionally, at social meetings, when the vexed question of the future of the colored race comes up, as it often does, for discussion, Mr. Clayton may still be heard to remark sententiously : —

"What the white people of the United States need most, in dealing with this problem, is a higher conception of the brotherhood of man. For of one blood God made all the nations of the earth."

CICELY'S DREAM

I

THE old woman stood at the back door of the cabin, shading her eyes with her hand, and looking across the vegetable garden that ran up to the very door. Beyond the garden she saw, bathed in the sunlight, a field of corn, just in the ear, stretching for half a mile, its yellow, pollen-laden tassels overtopping the dark green mass of broad glistening blades; and in the distance, through the faint morning haze of evaporating dew, the line of the woods, of a still darker green, meeting the clear blue of the summer sky. Old Dinah saw, going down the path, a tall, brown girl, in a homespun frock, swinging a slat-bonnet in one hand and a splint basket in the other.

"Oh, Cicely!" she called.

The girl turned and answered in a resonant voice, vibrating with youth and life, —

"Yes, granny!"

" Be sho' and pick a good mess er peas,
chile, fer yo' gran'daddy 's gwine ter be home
ter dinner ter-day."

The old woman stood a moment longer and
then turned to go into the house. What she
had not seen was that the girl was not only
young, but lithe and shapely as a sculptor's
model; that her bare feet seemed to spurn
the earth as they struck it; that though
brown, she was not so brown but that her
cheek was darkly red with the blood of another race than that which gave her her name
and station in life; and the old woman did not
see that Cicely's face was as comely as her
figure was superb, and that her eyes were
dreamy with vague yearnings.

Cicely climbed the low fence between the
garden and the cornfield, and started down
one of the long rows leading directly away
from the house. Old Needham was a good
ploughman, and straight as an arrow ran the
furrow between the rows of corn, until it vanished in the distant perspective. The peas
were planted beside alternate hills of corn, the
corn-stalks serving as supports for the climb-
ing pea-vines. The vines nearest the house
had been picked more or less clear of the long

green pods, and Cicely walked down the row
for a quarter of a mile, to where the peas were
more plentiful. And as she walked she
thought of her dream of the night before.

She had dreamed a beautiful dream. The
fact that it was a beautiful dream, a delightful dream, her memory retained very vividly.
She was troubled because she could not
remember just what her dream had been
about. Of one other fact she was certain, that
in her dream she had found something, and
that her happiness had been bound up with the
thing she had found. As she walked down the
corn-row she ran over in her mind the various
things with which she had always associated
happiness. Had she found a gold ring? No,
it was not a gold ring — of that she felt sure.
Was it a soft, curly plume for her hat?
She had seen town people with them, and
had indulged in day-dreams on the subject;
but it was not a feather. Was it a bright-
colored silk dress? No; as much as she had
always wanted one, it was not a silk dress.
For an instant, in a dream, she had tasted
some great and novel happiness, and when
she awoke it was dashed from her lips, and
she could not even enjoy the memory of it,

except in a vague, indefinite, and tantalizing
way.

Cicely was troubled, too, because dreams
were serious things. Dreams had certain
meanings, most of them, and some dreams
went by contraries. If her dream had been
a prophecy of some good thing, she had by
forgetting it lost the pleasure of anticipation. If her dream had been one of those
that go by contraries, the warning would be
in vain, because she would not know against
what evil to provide. So, with a sigh, Cicely
said to herself that it was a troubled world,
more or less ; and having come to a promising
point, began to pick the tenderest pea-pods
and throw them into her basket.

By the time she had reached the end of the
line the basket was nearly full. Glancing
toward the pine woods beyond the rail fence,
she saw a brier bush loaded with large,
luscious blackberries. Cicely was fond of
blackberries, so she set her basket down,
climbed the fence, and was soon busily engaged in gathering the fruit, delicious even
in its wild state.

She had soon eaten all she cared for. But
the berries were still numerous, and it occurred

to her that her granddaddy would like a black-
berry pudding for dinner. Catching up her
apron, and using it as a receptacle for the
berries, she had gathered scarcely more than
a handful when she heard a groan.

Cicely was not timid, and her curiosity
being aroused by the sound, she stood erect,
and remained in a listening attitude. In a
moment the sound was repeated, and, gaug-
ing the point from which it came, she plunged
resolutely into the thick underbrush of the
forest. She had gone but a few yards when
she stopped short with an exclamation of
surprise and concern.

Upon the ground, under the shadow of the
towering pines, a man lay at full length, —
a young man, several years under thirty, apparently, so far as his age could be guessed
from a face that wore a short soft beard,
and was so begrimed with dust and in-
crusted with blood that little could be seen of
the underlying integument. What was visible showed a skin browned by nature or by
exposure. His hands were of even a darker
brown, almost as dark as Cicely's own. A
tangled mass of very curly black hair, matted
with burs, dank with dew, and clotted with

blood, fell partly over his forehead, on the
edge of which, extending back into the hair,
an ugly scalp wound was gaping, and, though
apparently not just inflicted, was still bleeding
slowly, as though reluctant to stop, in spite
of the coagulation that had almost closed it.

Cicely with a glance took in all this and
more. But, first of all, she saw the man was
wounded and bleeding, and the nurse latent
in all womankind awoke in her to the require-
ments of the situation. She knew there was
a spring a few rods away, and ran swiftly
to it. There was usually a gourd at the
spring, but now it was gone. Pouring out
the blackberries in a little heap where they
could be found again, she took off her
apron, dipped one end of it into the spring,
and ran back to the wounded man. The
apron was clean, and she squeezed a little
stream of water from it into the man's
mouth. He swallowed it with avidity. Cicely
then knelt by his side, and with the wet
end of her apron washed the blood from
the wound lightly, and the dust from the
man's face. Then she looked at her apron a
moment, debating whether she should tear it
or not.

"I'm feared granny 'll be mad," she said to herself. "I reckon I'll jes' use de whole apron."

So she bound the apron around his head as well as she could, and then sat down a moment on a fallen tree trunk, to think what she should do next. The man already seemed more comfortable; he had ceased moaning, and lay quiet, though breathing heavily.

"What shall I do with that man?" she reflected. "I don' know whether he's a w'ite man or a black man. Ef he's a w'ite man, I oughter go an' tell de w'ite folks up at de big house, an' dey'd take keer of 'im. If he's a black man, I oughter go tell granny. He don' look lack a black man somehow er nuther, an' yet he don' look lack a w'ite man; he's too dahk, an' his hair's too curly. But I mus' do somethin' wid 'im. He can't be lef' here ter die in de woods all by hisse'f. Reckon I'll go an' tell granny."

She scaled the fence, caught up the basket of peas from where she had left it, and ran, lightly and swiftly as a deer, toward the house. Her short skirt did not impede her progress, and in a few minutes she had

covered the half mile and was at the cabin
door, a slight heaving of her full and yet
youthful breast being the only sign of any
unusual exertion.

Her story was told in a moment. The old
woman took down a black bottle from a high
shelf, and set out with Cicely across the cornfield, toward the wounded man.

As they went through the corn Cicely recalled part of her dream. She had dreamed
that under some strange circumstances — what
they had been was still obscure — she had met
a young man — a young man whiter than she
and yet not all white — and that he had loved
her and courted her and married her. Her
dream had been all the sweeter because in it
she had first tasted the sweetness of love, and
she had not recalled it before because only in
her dream had she known or thought of love
as something supremely desirable.

With the memory of her dream, however, her fears revived. Dreams were solemn things. To Cicely the fabric of a vision
was by no means baseless. Her trouble arose
from her not being able to recall, though she
was well versed in dream-lore, just what event
was foreshadowed by a dream of finding a

wounded man. If the wounded man were of her own race, her dream would thus far have been realized, and having met the young man, the other joys might be expected to follow. If he should turn out to be a white man, then her dream was clearly one of the kind that go by contraries, and she could expect only sorrow and trouble and pain as the proper sequences of this fateful discovery.

II

The two women reached the fence that separated the cornfield from the pine woods.

" How is I gwine ter git ovuh dat fence, chile? " asked the old woman.

" Wait a minute, granny," said Cicely; " I 'll take it down."

It was only an eight-rail fence, and it was a matter of but a few minutes for the girl to lift down and lay to either side the ends of the rails that formed one of the angles. This done, the old woman easily stepped across the remaining two or three rails. It was only a moment before they stood by the wounded man. He was lying still, breathing regularly, and seemingly asleep.

"What is he, granny," asked the girl anxiously, "a w'ite man, or not?"

Old Dinah pushed back the matted hair from the wounded man's brow, and looked at the skin beneath. It was fairer there, but yet of a decided brown. She raised his hand, pushed back the tattered sleeve from his wrist, and then she laid his hand down gently.

"Mos' lackly he's a mulatter man f'om up de country somewhar. He don' look lack dese yer niggers roun' yere, ner yet lack a w'ite man. But de po' boy's in a bad fix, w'ateber he is, an' I 'spec's we bettah do w'at we kin fer 'im, an' w'en he comes to he'll tell us w'at he is — er w'at he calls hisse'f. Hol' 'is head up, chile, an' I'll po' a drop er dis yer liquor down his th'oat; dat'll bring 'im to quicker 'n anything e'se I knows."

Cicely lifted the sick man's head, and Dinah poured a few drops of the whiskey between his teeth. He swallowed it readily enough. In a few minutes he opened his eyes and stared blankly at the two women. Cicely saw that his eyes were large and black, and glistening with fever.

"How you feelin', suh?" asked the old woman.

There was no answer.

" Is you feelin' bettah now ? "

The wounded man kept on staring blankly. Suddenly he essayed to put his hand to his head, gave a deep groan, and fell back again unconscious.

" He 's gone ag'in," said Dinah.   " I reckon we 'll hafter tote 'im up ter de house and take keer er 'im dere.   W'ite folks would n't want ter fool wid a nigger man, an' we doan know who his folks is.   He 's outer his head an' will be fer some time yet, an' we can't tell nuthin' 'bout 'im tel he comes ter his senses."

Cicely lifted the wounded man by the arms and shoulders.   She was strong, with the strength of youth and a sturdy race.   The man was pitifully emaciated ; how much, the two women had not suspected until they raised him.   They had no difficulty whatever, except for the awkwardness of such a burden, in lifting him over the fence and carrying him through the cornfield to the cabin.

They laid him on Cicely's bed in the little lean-to shed that formed a room separate from the main apartment of the cabin.   The old woman sent Cicely to cook the dinner, while she gave her own attention exclusively to the still unconscious man. She brought water and washed him as though he were a child.

"Po' boy," she said, "he doan feel lack he's be'n eatin' nuff to feed a sparrer. He 'pears ter be mos' starved ter def."

She washed his wound more carefully, made some lint, — the art was well known in the sixties, — and dressed his wound with a fair degree of skill.

"Somebody must 'a' be'n tryin' ter put yo' light out, chile," she muttered to herself as she adjusted the bandage around his head. "A little higher er a little lower, an' you would n' 'a' be'n yere ter tell de tale. Dem clo's," she argued, lifting the tattered garments she had removed from her patient, "don' b'long 'roun' yere. Dat kinder weavin' come f'om down to'ds Souf Ca'lina. I wish Needham 'u'd come erlong. He kin tell who dis man is, an' all erbout 'im."

She made a bowl of gruel, and fed it, drop by drop, to the sick man. This roused him somewhat from his stupor, but when Dinah thought he had enough of the gruel, and stopped feeding him, he closed his eyes again and relapsed into a heavy sleep that was so closely akin to unconsciousness as to be scarcely distinguishable from it.

When old Needham came home at noon, his wife, who had been anxiously awaiting his return, told him in a few words the story of Cicely's discovery and of the subsequent events.

Needham inspected the stranger with a professional eye. He had been something of a plantation doctor in his day, and was known far and wide for his knowledge of simple remedies. The negroes all around, as well as many of the poorer white people, came to him for the treatment of common ailments.

"He 's got a fevuh," he said, after feeling the patient's pulse and laying his hand on his brow, "an' we 'll hafter gib 'im some yarb tea an' nuss 'im tel de fevuh w'ars off. I 'spec'," he added, "dat I knows whar dis boy come f'om. He 's mos' lackly one er dem bright mulatters, f'om Robeson County — some of 'em call deyse'ves Croatan Injins — w'at's been conscripted an' sent ter wu'k on de fo'tifications down at Wimbleton er some- 'er's er nuther, an' done 'scaped, and got mos' killed gittin' erway, an' wuz n' none too well fed befo', an' nigh 'bout starved ter def sence.

We 'll hafter hide dis man, er e'se we is
lackly ter git inter trouble ou'se'ves by harb'-
rin' 'im. Ef dey ketch 'im yere, dey's liable
ter take 'im out an' shoot 'im — an' des ez
lackly us too."

Cicely was listening with bated breath.

"Oh, gran'daddy," she cried with trembling voice, "don' let 'em ketch 'im ! Hide
'im somewhar."

"I reckon we 'll leave 'im yere fer a day er
so. Ef he had come f'om roun' yere I 'd be
skeered ter keep 'im, fer de w'ite folks 'u'd
prob'ly be lookin' fer 'im. But I knows ev'y-
body w'at 's be'n conscripted fer ten miles
'roun', an' dis yere boy don' b'long in dis
neighborhood. W'en 'e gits so 'e kin he'p
'isse'f we'll put 'im up in de lof' an' hide 'im
till de Yankees come. Fer dey 're comin',
sho'. I dremp' las' night dey wuz close ter
han', and I hears de w'ite folks talkin' ter
deyse'ves 'bout it. An' de time is comin'
w'en de good Lawd gwine ter set his people
free, an' it ain' gwine ter be long, nuther."

Needham's prophecy proved true. In less
than a week the Confederate garrison evacu-
ated the arsenal in the neighboring town of
Patesville, blew up the buildings, destroyed

the ordnance and stores, and retreated across
the Cape Fear River, burning the river bridge
behind them, — two acts of war afterwards
unjustly attributed to General Sherman's
army, which followed close upon the heels
of the retreating Confederates.

When there was no longer any fear for
the stranger's safety, no more pains were
taken to conceal him. His wound had healed
rapidly, and in a week he had been able with
some help to climb up the ladder into the
loft. In all this time, however, though apparently conscious, he had said no word to any
one, nor had he seemed to comprehend a
word that was spoken to him.

Cicely had been his constant attendant.
After the first day, during which her granny
had nursed him, she had sat by his bedside,
had fanned his fevered brow, had held food
and water and medicine to his lips. When it
was safe for him to come down from the loft
and sit in a chair under a spreading oak,
Cicely supported him until he was strong
enough to walk about the yard. When his
strength had increased sufficiently to permit
of greater exertion, she accompanied him on
long rambles in the fields and woods.

In spite of his gain in physical strength, the newcomer changed very little in other respects. For a long time he neither spoke nor smiled. To questions put to him he simply gave no reply, but looked at his questioner with the blank unconsciousness of an infant. By and by he began to recognize Cicely, and to smile at her approach. The next step in returning consciousness was but another manifestation of the same sentiment. When Cicely would leave him he would look his regret, and be restless and uneasy until she returned.

The family were at a loss what to call him. To any inquiry as to his name he answered no more than to other questions.

" He come jes' befo' Sherman," said Needham, after a few weeks, "lack John de Baptis' befo' de Lawd. I reckon we bettah call 'im John."

So they called him John. He soon learned the name. As time went on Cicely found that he was quick at learning things. She taught him to speak her own negro English, which he pronounced with absolute fidelity to her intonations; so that barring the quality of his voice, his speech was an echo of Cicely's own.

The summer wore away and the autumn came. John and Cicely wandered in the woods together and gathered walnuts, and chinquapins and wild grapes. When harvest time came, they worked in the fields side by side, — plucked the corn, pulled the fodder, and gathered the dried peas from the yellow pea-vines. Cicely was a phenomenal cotton-picker, and John accompanied her to the fields and stayed by her hours at a time, though occasionally he would complain of his head, and sit under a tree and rest part of the day while Cicely worked, the two keeping one another always in sight.

They did not have a great deal of inter-course with other people. Young men came to the cabin sometimes to see Cicely, but when they found her entirely absorbed in the stranger they ceased their visits. For a time Cicely kept him away, as much as possible, from others, because she did not wish them to see that there was anything wrong about him. This was her motive at first, but after a while she kept him to herself simply because she was happier so. He was hers — hers alone. She had found him, as Pharaoh's daughter had found Moses in the bulrushes; she had

taught him to speak, to think, to love. She
had not taught him to remember; she would
not have wished him to; she would have been
jealous of any past to which he might have
proved bound by other ties. Her dream so
far had come true. She had found him; he
loved her. The rest of it would as surely follow, and that before long. For dreams were
serious things, and time had proved hers to
have been not a presage of misfortune, but
one of the beneficent visions that are sent,
that we may enjoy by anticipation the good
things that are in store for us.

III

But a short interval of time elapsed after
the passage of the warlike host that swept
through North Carolina, until there appeared
upon the scene the vanguard of a second
army, which came to bring light and the
fruits of liberty to a land which slavery and
the havoc of war had brought to ruin. It is
fashionable to assume that those who under-
took the political rehabilitation of the Southern States merely rounded out the ruin that
the war had wrought — merely ploughed up

the desolate land and sowed it with salt.
Perhaps the gentler judgments of the future
may recognize that their task was a difficult
one, and that wiser and honester men might
have failed as egregiously.   It may even, in
time, be conceded that some good came out of
the carpet-bag governments, as, for instance,
the establishment of a system of popular education in the former slave States.   Where it
had been a crime to teach people to read or
write, a schoolhouse dotted every hillside, and
the State provided education for rich and
poor, for white and black alike.   Let us lay
at least this token upon the grave of the car-
pet-baggers.   The evil they did lives after
them, and the statute of limitations does not
seem to run against it.   It is but just that
we should not forget the good.

Long, however, before the work of political
reconstruction had begun, a brigade of Yankee
schoolmasters and schoolma'ams had invaded
Dixie, and one of the latter had opened a
Freedman's Bureau School in the town of
Patesville, about four miles from Needham
Green's cabin on the neighboring sandhills.

It had been quite a surprise to Miss Chandler's Boston friends when she had announced

her intention of going South to teach the
freedmen. Rich, accomplished, beautiful, and
a social favorite, she was giving up the com-
forts and luxuries of Northern life to go
among hostile strangers, where her associates
would be mostly ignorant negroes. Perhaps
she might meet occasionally an officer of some
Federal garrison, or a traveler from the North ;
but to all intents and purposes her friends
considered her as going into voluntary exile.
But heroism was not rare in those days, and
Martha Chandler was only one of the great
multitude whose hearts went out toward an
oppressed race, and who freely poured out
their talents, their money, their lives, — whatever God had given them, — in the sublime
and not unfruitful effort to transform three
millions of slaves into intelligent freemen.
Miss Chandler's friends knew, too, that she
had met a great sorrow, and more than suspected that out of it had grown her determination to go South.

When Cicely Green heard that a school for
colored people had been opened at Patesville
she combed her hair, put on her Sunday frock
and such bits of finery as she possessed, and
set out for town early the next Monday morning.

There were many who came to learn the
new gospel of education, which was to be the
cure for all the freedmen's ills.   The old and
gray-haired, the full-grown man and woman,
the toddling infant, — they came to acquire
the new and wonderful learning that was to
make them the equals of the white people.
It was the teacher's task, by no means an easy
one, to select from this incongruous mass the
most promising material, and to distribute
among them the second-hand books and clothing that were sent, largely by her Boston
friends, to aid her in her work; to find out
what they knew, to classify them by their
intelligence rather than by their knowledge,
for they were all lamentably ignorant.   Some
among them were the children of parents who
had been free before the war, and of these
some few could read and one or two could
write.   One paragon, who could repeat the
multiplication table, was immediately pro-
moted to the position of pupil teacher.

Miss Chandler took a liking to the tall girl
who had come so far to sit under her instruction.   There was a fine, free air in her bearing, a lightness in her step, a sparkle in her
eye, that spoke of good blood, — whether

fused by nature in its own alembic, out of
material despised and spurned of men, or
whether some obscure ancestral strain, the
teacher could not tell. The girl proved intelligent and learned rapidly, indeed seemed
almost feverishly anxious to learn. She was
quiet, and was, though utterly untrained, instinctively polite, and profited from the first
day by the example of her teacher's quiet ele-
gance. The teacher dressed in simple black.
When Cicely came back to school the second
day, she had left off her glass beads and her
red ribbon, and had arranged her hair as
nearly like the teacher's as her skill and its
quality would permit.

The teacher was touched by these efforts
at imitation, and by the intense devotion
Cicely soon manifested toward her. It was
not a sycophantic, troublesome devotion, that
made itself a burden to its object. It found
expression in little things done rather than
in any words the girl said. To the degree
that the attraction was mutual, Martha recognized in it a sort of freemasonry of temperament that drew them together in spite
of the differences between them. Martha
felt sometimes, in the vague way that one

speculates about the impossible, that if she were brown, and had been brought up in North Carolina, she would be like Cicely; and that if Cicely's ancestors had come over in the Mayflower, and Cicely had been reared on Beacon Street, in the shadow of the State House dome, Cicely would have been very much like herself.

Miss Chandler was lonely sometimes. Her duties kept her occupied all day. On Sundays she taught a Bible class in the school-room. Correspondence with bureau officials and friends at home furnished her with additional occupation. At times, nevertheless, she felt a longing for the company of women of her own race; but the white ladies of the town did not call, even in the most formal way, upon the Yankee school-teacher. Miss Chandler was therefore fain to do the best she could with such companionship as was available. She took Cicely to her home occasionally, and asked her once to stay all night. Thinking, however, that she detected a reluctance on the girl's part to remain away from home, she did not repeat her invitation.

Cicely, indeed, was filling a double rôle.

The learning acquired from Miss Chandler she imparted to John at home. Every evening, by the light of the pine-knots blazing on Needham's ample hearth, she taught John to read the simple words she had learned during the day. Why she did not take him to school she had never asked herself; there were several other pupils as old as he seemed to be. Perhaps she still thought it necessary to protect him from curious remark. He worked with Needham by day, and she could see him at night, and all of Saturdays and Sundays. Perhaps it was the jealous selfishness of love. She had found him; he was hers. In the spring, when school was over, her granny had said that she might marry him. Till then her dream would not yet have come true, and she must keep him to herself. And yet she did not wish him to lose this golden key to the avenues of opportunity. She would not take him to school, but she would teach him each day all that she herself had learned. He was not difficult to teach, but learned, indeed, with what seemed to Cicely marvelous ease, — always, however, by her lead, and never of his own initiative. For while he could do a man's work, he was in most things but a child,

without a child's curiosity. His love for
Cicely appeared the only thing for which he
needed no suggestion; and even that possessed an element of childish dependence
that would have seemed, to minds trained to
thoughtful observation, infinitely pathetic.

The spring came and cotton-planting time.
The children began to drop out of Miss
Chandler's school one by one, as their services
were required at home. Cicely was among
those who intended to remain in school until
the term closed with the " exhibition," in
which she was assigned a leading part. She
had selected her recitation, or " speech,"
from among half a dozen poems that her
teacher had suggested, and to memorizing it
she devoted considerable time and study.
The exhibition, as the first of its kind, was
sure to be a notable event. The parents and
friends of the children were invited to attend,
and a colored church, recently erected, — the
largest available building, — was secured as
the place where the exercises should take
place.

On the morning of the eventful day, uncle
Needham, assisted by John, harnessed the
mule to the two-wheeled cart, on which a

couple of splint-bottomed chairs were fastened
to accommodate Dinah and Cicely. John put
on his best clothes, — an ill-fitting suit of
blue jeans, — a round wool hat, a pair of
coarse brogans, a homespun shirt, and a
bright blue necktie. Cicely wore her best
frock, a red ribbon at her throat, another in
her hair, and carried a bunch of flowers in
her hand. Uncle Needham and aunt Dinah
were also in holiday array. Needham and
John took their seats on opposite sides of the
cart-frame, with their feet dangling down,
and thus the equipage set out leisurely for
the town.

Cicely had long looked forward impatiently
to this day. She was going to marry John
the next week, and then her dream would
have come entirely true. But even this anticipated happiness did not overshadow the
importance of the present occasion, which
would be an epoch in her life, a day of joy
and triumph. She knew her speech perfectly, and timidity was not one of her weak-
nesses. She knew that the red ribbons set
off her dark beauty effectively, and that her
dress fitted neatly the curves of her shapely
figure. She confidently expected to win the

first prize, a large morocco-covered Bible, offered by Miss Chandler for the best exercise.

Cicely and her companions soon arrived at Patesville. Their entrance into the church made quite a sensation, for Cicely was not only an acknowledged belle, but a general favorite, and to John there attached a tinge of mystery which inspired a respect not bestowed upon those who had grown up in the neighborhood. Cicely secured a seat in the front part of the church, next to the aisle, in the place reserved for the pupils. As the house was already partly filled by townspeople when the party from the country arrived, Needham and his wife and John were forced to content themselves with places somewhat in the rear of the room, from which they could see and hear what took place on the platform, but where they were not at all conspicuously visible to those at the front of the church.

The schoolmistress had not yet arrived, and order was preserved in the audience by two of the elder pupils, adorned with large rosettes of red, white, and blue, who ushered the most important visitors to the seats

reserved for them. A national flag was
gracefully draped over the platform, and
under it hung a lithograph of the Great
Emancipator, for it was thus these people
thought of him. He had saved the Union,
but the Union had never meant anything
good to them. He had proclaimed liberty to
the captive, which meant all to them; and to
them he was and would ever be the Great
Emancipator.

The schoolmistress came in at a rear door
and took her seat upon the platform. Martha
was dressed in white; for once she had laid
aside the sombre garb in which alone she had
been seen since her arrival at Patesville. She
wore a yellow rose at her throat, a bunch of
jasmine in her belt. A sense of responsibility for the success of the exhibition had
deepened the habitual seriousness of her face,
yet she greeted the audience with a smile.

" Don' Miss Chan'ler look sweet," whispered the little girls to one another, devour-
ing her beauty with sparkling eyes, their lips
parted over a wealth of ivory.

" De Lawd will bress dat chile," said one
old woman, in soliloquy. " I t'ank de good
Marster I 's libbed ter see dis day."

Even envy could not hide its noisome head : a pretty quadroon whispered to her neighbor : —

"I don't b'liebe she's natch'ly ez white ez dat. I 'spec' she's be'n powd'rin'! An' I know all dat hair can't be her'n; she's got on a switch, sho's you bawn."

"You knows dat ain' so, Ma'y 'Liza Smif," rejoined the other, with a look of stern disapproval; "you *knows* dat ain' so. You'd gib yo' everlastin' soul 'f you wuz ez white ez Miss Chan'ler, en yo' ha'r wuz ez long ez her'n."

"By Jove, Maxwell!" exclaimed a young officer, who belonged to the Federal garrison stationed in the town, "but that girl is a beauty." The speaker and a companion were in fatigue uniform, and had merely dropped in for an hour between garrison duty. The ushers had wished to give them seats on the platform, but they had declined, thinking that perhaps their presence there might embarrass the teacher. They sought rather to avoid observation by sitting behind a pillar in the rear of the room, around which they could see without attracting undue attention.

"To think," the lieutenant went on, "of

that Junonian figure, those lustrous orbs, that golden coronal, that flower of Northern civilization, being wasted on these barbarians!" The speaker uttered an exaggerated but suppressed groan.

His companion, a young man of clean-shaven face and serious aspect, nodded assent, but whispered reprovingly, —

"'Sh! some one will hear you. The exercises are going to begin."

When Miss Chandler stepped forward to announce the hymn to be sung by the school as the first exercise, every eye in the room was fixed upon her, except John's, which saw only Cicely. When the teacher had uttered a few words, he looked up to her, and from that moment did not take his eyes off Martha's face.

After the singing, a little girl, dressed in white, crossed by ribbons of red and blue, recited with much spirit a patriotic poem.

When Martha announced the third exercise, John's face took on a more than usually animated expression, and there was a perceptible deepening of the troubled look in his eyes, never entirely absent since Cicely had found him in the woods.

A little yellow boy, with long curls, and a frightened air, next ascended the platform.

"Now, Jimmie, be a man, and speak right out," whispered his teacher, tapping his arm reassuringly with her fan as he passed her.

Jimmie essayed to recite the lines so familiar to a past generation of schoolchildren : —

> "I knew a widow very poor,
> Who four small children had ;
> The eldest was but six years old,
> A gentle, modest lad."

He ducked his head hurriedly in a futile attempt at a bow; then, following instructions previously given him, fixed his eyes upon a large cardboard motto hanging on the rear wall of the room, which admonished him in bright red letters to

"ALWAYS SPEAK THE TRUTH,"

and started off with assumed confidence —

> "I knew a widow very poor,
> Who" —

At this point, drawn by an irresistible impulse, his eyes sought the level of the audience. Ah, fatal blunder ! He stammered, but with an effort raised his eyes and began again :

> "I knew a widow very poor,
>   Who four " —

Again his treacherous eyes fell, and his little
remaining self-possession utterly forsook him.
He made one more despairing effort : —

> "I knew a widow very poor,
>   Who four small " —

and then, bursting into tears, turned and
fled amid a murmur of sympathy.

Jimmie's inglorious retreat was covered by
the singing in chorus of " The Star-spangled
Banner," after which Cicely Green came forward to recite her poem.

" By Jove, Maxwell ! " whispered the young
officer, who was evidently a connoisseur of
female beauty, " that is n't bad for a bronze
Venus. I 'll tell you " —

" 'Sh ! " said the other. " Keep still."

When Cicely finished her recitation, the
young officers began to applaud, but stopped
suddenly in some confusion as they realized
that they were the only ones in the audience
so engaged. The colored people had either
not learned how to express their approval in
orthodox fashion, or else their respect for the
sacred character of the edifice forbade any
such demonstration. Their enthusiasm found

vent, however, in a subdued murmur, emphasized by numerous nods and winks and suppressed exclamations. During the singing that followed Cicely's recitation the two officers quietly withdrew, their duties calling them away at this hour.

At the close of the exercises, a committee on prizes met in the vestibule, and unanimously decided that Cicely Green was entitled to the first prize. Proudly erect, with sparkling eyes and cheeks flushed with victory, Cicely advanced to the platform to receive the coveted reward. As she turned away, her eyes, shining with gratified vanity, sought those of her lover.

John sat bent slightly forward in an attitude of strained attention; and Cicely's triumph lost half its value when she saw that it was not at her, but at Miss Chandler, that his look was directed. Though she watched him thenceforward, not one glance did he vouchsafe to his jealous sweetheart, and never for an instant withdrew his eyes from Martha, or relaxed the unnatural intentness of his gaze. The imprisoned mind, stirred to unwonted effort, was struggling for liberty; and from Martha had come the first ray of outer light that had penetrated its dungeon.

Before the audience was dismissed, the teacher rose to bid her school farewell. Her intention was to take a vacation of three months; but what might happen in that time she did not know, and there were duties at home of such apparent urgency as to render her return to North Carolina at least doubtful; so that in her own heart her *au revoir* sounded very much like a farewell.

She spoke to them of the hopeful progress they had made, and praised them for their eager desire to learn. She told them of the serious duties of life, and of the use they should make of their acquirements. With prophetic finger she pointed them to the upward way which they must climb with patient feet to raise themselves out of the depths.

Then, an unusual thing with her, she spoke of herself. Her heart was full; it was with difficulty that she maintained her composure; for the faces that confronted her were kindly faces, and not critical, and some of them she had learned to love right well.

" I am going away from you, my children," she said; " but before I go I want to tell you how I came to be in North Carolina; so that if I have been able to do anything here among you for which you might feel inclined, in your good nature, to thank me, you may thank not me alone, but another who came before me, and whose work I have but taken up where *he* laid it down. I had a friend, — a dear friend, — why should I be ashamed to say it? — a lover, to whom I was to be married, — as I hope all you girls may some day be happily married. His country needed him, and I gave him up. He came to fight for the Union and for Freedom, for he believed that all men are brothers. He did not come back again — he gave up his life for you. Could I do less than he? I came to the land that he sanctified by his death, and I have tried in my weak way to tend the plant he watered with his blood, and which, in the fullness of time, will blossom forth into the perfect flower of liberty."

She could say no more, and as the whole audience thrilled in sympathy with her emotion, there was a hoarse cry from the men's side of the room, and John forced his way to the aisle and rushed forward to the platform.

" Martha ! Martha ! "

" Arthur ! O Arthur ! "

Pent-up love burst the flood-gates of de-

spair and oblivion, and caught these two young
hearts in its torrent. Captain Arthur Carey,
of the 1st Massachusetts, long since reported
missing, and mourned as dead, was restored to
reason and to his world.

It seemed to him but yesterday that he had
escaped from the Confederate prison at Salis-
bury ; that in an encounter with a guard he
had received a wound in the head ; that he
had wandered on in the woods, keeping himself alive by means of wild berries, with now
and then a piece of bread or a potato from a
friendly negro. It seemed but the night before that he had laid himself down, tortured
with fever, weak from loss of blood, and with
no hope that he would ever rise again. From
that moment his memory of the past was a
blank until he recognized Martha on the platform and took up again the thread of his former existence where it had been broken off.

And Cicely ? Well, there is often another
woman, and Cicely, all unwittingly to Carey
or to Martha, had been the other woman.
For, after all, her beautiful dream had been
one of the kind that go by contraries.

THE PASSING OF GRANDISON

I

WHEN it is said that it was done to please a woman, there ought perhaps to be enough said to explain anything; for what a man will not do to please a woman is yet to be discovered. Nevertheless, it might be well to state a few preliminary facts to make it clear why young Dick Owens tried to run one of his father's negro men off to Canada.

In the early fifties, when the growth of anti-slavery sentiment and the constant drain of fugitive slaves into the North had so alarmed the slaveholders of the border States as to lead to the passage of the Fugitive Slave Law, a young white man from Ohio, moved by compassion for the sufferings of a certain bondman who happened to have a "hard master," essayed to help the slave to freedom. The attempt was discovered and frustrated; the abductor was tried and convicted for slave-stealing, and sentenced to a term of imprison-

ment in the penitentiary. His death, after
the expiration of only a small part of the
sentence, from cholera contracted while nurs-
ing stricken fellow prisoners, lent to the case
a melancholy interest that made it famous in
anti-slavery annals.

Dick Owens had attended the trial. He
was a youth of about twenty-two, intelligent,
handsome, and amiable, but extremely indolent, in a graceful and gentlemanly way ; or,
as old Judge Fenderson put it more than
once, he was lazy as the Devil, — a mere figure
of speech, of course, and not one that did
justice to the Enemy of Mankind. When
asked why he never did anything serious,
Dick would good-naturedly reply, with a well-
modulated drawl, that he did n't have to. His
father was rich ; there was but one other
child, an unmarried daughter, who because of
poor health would probably never marry, and
Dick was therefore heir presumptive to a large
estate. Wealth or social position he did not
need to seek, for he was born to both. Charity Lomax had shamed him into studying law,
but notwithstanding an hour or so a day spent
at old Judge Fenderson's office, he did not
make remarkable headway in his legal studies.

"What Dick needs," said the judge, who was fond of tropes, as became a scholar, and of horses, as was befitting a Kentuckian, "is the whip of necessity, or the spur of ambition. If he had either, he would soon need the snaffle to hold him back."

But all Dick required, in fact, to prompt him to the most remarkable thing he accomplished before he was twenty-five, was a mere suggestion from Charity Lomax. The story was never really known to but two persons until after the war, when it came out because it was a good story and there was no particular reason for its concealment.

Young Owens had attended the trial of this slave-stealer, or martyr, — either or both, — and, when it was over, had gone to call on Charity Lomax, and, while they sat on the veranda after sundown, had told her all about the trial. He was a good talker, as his career in later years disclosed, and described the proceedings very graphically.

"I confess," he admitted, "that while my principles were against the prisoner, my sympathies were on his side. It appeared that he was of good family, and that he had an old father and mother, respectable people, depend-

ent upon him for support and comfort in their
declining years.   He had been led into the
matter by pity for a negro whose master ought
to have been run out of the county long ago
for abusing his slaves.   If it had been merely
a question of old Sam Briggs's negro, nobody
would have cared anything about it.   But
father and the rest of them stood on the principle of the thing, and told the judge so, and
the fellow was sentenced to three years in the
penitentiary."

Miss Lomax had listened with lively interest.

" I 've always hated old Sam Briggs," she
said emphatically, " ever since the time he
broke a negro's leg with a piece of cordwood.
When I hear of a cruel deed it makes the
Quaker blood that came from my grandmo-
ther assert itself.   Personally I wish that all
Sam Briggs's negroes would run away.   As for
the young man, I regard him as a hero.   He
dared something for humanity.   I could love
a man who would take such chances for the
sake of others."

" Could you love me, Charity, if I did
something heroic ? "

" You never will, Dick.   You 're too lazy

for any use. You'll never do anything
harder than playing cards or fox-hunting."

"Oh, come now, sweetheart! I've been
courting you for a year, and it's the hardest
work imaginable. Are you never going to
love me?" he pleaded.

His hand sought hers, but she drew it
back beyond his reach.

"I'll never love you, Dick Owens, until
you have done something. When that time
comes, I'll think about it."

"But it takes so long to do anything worth
mentioning, and I don't want to wait. One
must read two years to become a lawyer, and
work five more to make a reputation. We
shall both be gray by then."

"Oh, I don't know," she rejoined. "It
does n't require a lifetime for a man to prove
that he is a man. This one did something,
or at least tried to."

"Well, I'm willing to attempt as much as
any other man. What do you want me to
do, sweetheart? Give me a test."

"Oh, dear me!" said Charity, "I don't
care what you *do*, so you do *something*.
Really, come to think of it, why should I
care whether you do anything or not?"

"I'm sure I don't know why you should, Charity," rejoined Dick humbly, "for I'm aware that I'm not worthy of it."

"Except that I do hate," she added, relenting slightly, "to see a really clever man so utterly lazy and good for nothing."

"Thank you, my dear; a word of praise from you has sharpened my wits already. I have an idea! Will you love me if *I* run a negro off to Canada?"

"What nonsense!" said Charity scornfully. "You must be losing your wits. Steal another man's slave, indeed, while your father owns a hundred!"

"Oh, there'll be no trouble about that," responded Dick lightly; "I'll run off one of the old man's; we've got too many anyway. It may not be quite as difficult as the other man found it, but it will be just as unlawful, and will demonstrate what I am capable of."

"Seeing's believing," replied Charity. "Of course, what you are talking about now is merely absurd. I'm going away for three weeks, to visit my aunt in Tennessee. If you're able to tell me, when I return, that you've done something to prove your quality, I'll — well, you may come and tell me about it."

II

Young Owens got up about nine o'clock next morning, and while making his toilet put some questions to his personal attendant, a rather bright looking young mulatto of about his own age.

" Tom," said Dick.

" Yas, Mars Dick," responded the servant.

" I 'm going on a trip North.   Would you like to go with me ? "

Now, if there was anything that Tom would have liked to make, it was a trip North. It was something he had long contemplated in the abstract, but had never been able to muster up sufficient courage to attempt in the concrete.   He was prudent enough, however, to dissemble his feelings.

" I would n't min' it, Mars Dick, ez long ez you 'd take keer er me an' fetch me home all right."

Tom's eyes belied his words, however, and his young master felt well assured that Tom needed only a good opportunity to make him run away.   Having a comfortable home, and a dismal prospect in case of failure, Tom was not likely to take any desperate chances ; but young Owens was satisfied that in a free State but little persuasion would be required to lead Tom astray. With a very logical and characteristic desire to gain his end with the least necessary expenditure of effort, he decided to take Tom with him, if his father did not object.

Colonel Owens had left the house when Dick went to breakfast, so Dick did not see his father till luncheon.

"Father," he remarked casually to the colonel, over the fried chicken, "I'm feeling a trifle run down. I imagine my health would be improved somewhat by a little travel and change of scene."

"Why don't you take a trip North?" suggested his father. The colonel added to paternal affection a considerable respect for his son as the heir of a large estate. He himself had been "raised" in comparative poverty, and had laid the foundations of his fortune by hard work; and while he despised the ladder by which he had climbed, he could not entirely forget it, and unconsciously manifested, in his intercourse with his son, some of the poor man's deference toward the wealthy and well-born.

"I think I'll adopt your suggestion, sir," replied the son, "and run up to New York; and after I've been there awhile I may go on to Boston for a week or so. I've never been there, you know."

"There are some matters you can talk over with my factor in New York," rejoined the colonel, "and while you are up there among the Yankees, I hope you'll keep your eyes and ears open to find out what the rascally abolitionists are saying and doing. They're becoming altogether too active for our comfort, and entirely too many ungrateful niggers are running away. I hope the conviction of that fellow yesterday may discourage the rest of the breed. I'd just like to catch any one trying to run off one of my darkeys. He'd get short shrift; I don't think any Court would have a chance to try him."

"They are a pestiferous lot," assented Dick, "and dangerous to our institutions. But say, father, if I go North I shall want to take Tom with me."

Now, the colonel, while a very indulgent father, had pronounced views on the subject of negroes, having studied them, as he often said, for a great many years, and, as he asserted oftener still, understanding them perfectly. It is scarcely worth while to say, either, that he valued more highly than if he had inherited them the slaves he had toiled and schemed for.

"I don't think it safe to take Tom up North," he declared, with promptness and decision. "He's a good enough boy, but too smart to trust among those low-down abolitionists. I strongly suspect him of having learned to read, though I can't imagine how. I saw him with a newspaper the other day, and while he pretended to be looking at a woodcut, I'm almost sure he was reading the paper. I think it by no means safe to take him."

Dick did not insist, because he knew it was useless. The colonel would have obliged his son in any other matter, but his negroes were the outward and visible sign of his wealth and station, and therefore sacred to him.

"Whom do you think it safe to take?" asked Dick. "I suppose I'll have to have a body-servant."

"What's the matter with Grandison?" suggested the colonel. "He's handy enough, and I reckon we can trust him. He's too fond of good eating, to risk losing his regular

meals; besides, he's sweet on your mother's
maid, Betty, and I've promised to let 'em get
married before long.   I'll have Grandison up,
and we'll talk to him.   Here, you boy Jack,"
called the colonel to a yellow youth in the
next room who was catching flies and pulling
their wings off to pass the time, " go down to
the barn and tell Grandison to come here."

" Grandison," said the colonel, when the
negro stood before him, hat in hand.

" Yas, marster."

" Have n't I always treated you right ? "

" Yas, marster."

" Have n't you always got all you wanted
to eat ? "

" Yas, marster."

" And as much whiskey and tobacco as was
good for you, Grandison ? "

" Y-a-s, marster."

" I should just like to know, Grandison,
whether you don't think yourself a great deal
better off than those poor free negroes down
by the plank road, with no kind master to
look after them and no mistress to give them
medicine when they're sick and — and "—

" Well, I sh'd jes' reckon I is better off,
suh, dan dem low-down free niggers, suh !

Ef anybody ax 'em who dey b'long ter, dey has ter say nobody, er e'se lie erbout it. Anybody ax me who I b'longs ter, I ain' got no 'casion ter be shame' ter tell 'em, no, suh, 'deed I ain', suh ! "

The colonel was beaming. This was true gratitude, and his feudal heart thrilled at such appreciative homage. What cold-blooded, heartless monsters they were who would break up this blissful relationship of kindly protection on the one hand, of wise subordination and loyal dependence on the other ! The colonel always became indignant at the mere thought of such wickedness.

" Grandison," the colonel continued, " your young master Dick is going North for a few weeks, and I am thinking of letting him take you along. I shall send you on this trip, Grandison, in order that you may take care of your young master. He will need some one to wait on him, and no one can ever do it so well as one of the boys brought up with him on the old plantation. I am going to trust him in your hands, and I'm sure you'll do your duty faithfully, and bring him back home safe and sound — to old Kentucky."

Grandison grinned. "Oh yas, marster, I'll take keer er young Mars Dick."

"I want to warn you, though, Grandison," continued the colonel impressively, "against these cussed abolitionists, who try to entice servants from their comfortable homes and their indulgent masters, from the blue skies, the green fields, and the warm sunlight of their southern home, and send them away off yonder to Canada, a dreary country, where the woods are full of wildcats and wolves and bears, where the snow lies up to the eaves of the houses for six months of the year, and the cold is so severe that it freezes your breath and curdles your blood; and where, when runaway niggers get sick and can't work, they are turned out to starve and die, unloved and uncared for. I reckon, Grandison, that you have too much sense to permit yourself to be led astray by any such foolish and wicked people."

"'Deed, suh, I would n' low none er dem cussed, low-down abolitioners ter come nigh me, suh. I'd — I'd — would I be 'lowed ter hit 'em, suh?"

"Certainly, Grandison," replied the colonel, chuckling, "hit 'em as hard as you can. I reckon they'd rather like it. Begad, I believe they would! It would serve 'em right to be hit by a nigger!"

"Er ef I didn't hit 'em, suh," continued Grandison reflectively, "I'd tell Mars Dick, en *he'd* fix 'em. He'd smash de face off'n 'em, suh, I jes' knows he would."

"Oh yes, Grandison, your young master will protect you. You need fear no harm while he is near."

"Dey won't try ter steal me, will dey, marster?" asked the negro, with sudden alarm.

"I don't know, Grandison," replied the colonel, lighting a fresh cigar. "They're a desperate set of lunatics, and there's no telling what they may resort to. But if you stick close to your young master, and remember always that he is your best friend, and understands your real needs, and has your true interests at heart, and if you will be careful to avoid strangers who try to talk to you, you'll stand a fair chance of getting back to your home and your friends. And if you please your master Dick, he'll buy you a present, and a string of beads for Betty to wear when you and she get married in the fall."

"Thanky, marster, thanky, suh," replied
Grandison, oozing gratitude at every pore;
"you is a good marster, to be sho', suh; yas,
'deed you is.   You kin jes' bet me and Mars
Dick gwine git 'long jes' lack I wuz own boy
ter Mars Dick.   En it won't be my fault ef
he don' want me fer his boy all de time, w'en
we come back home ag'in."

"All right, Grandison, you may go now.
You need n't work any more to-day, and
here 's a piece of tobacco for you off my own
plug."

"Thanky, marster, thanky, marster!   You
is de bes' marster any nigger ever had in dis
worl'."   And Grandison bowed and scraped
and disappeared round the corner, his jaws
closing around a large section of the colonel's
best tobacco.

"You may take Grandison," said the colonel to his son.   "I allow he 's abolitionist-
proof."

III

Richard Owens, Esq., and servant, from
Kentucky, registered at the fashionable New
York hostelry for Southerners in those days,
a hotel where an atmosphere congenial to

Southern institutions was sedulously maintained. But there were negro waiters in the
dining-room, and mulatto bell-boys, and Dick
had no doubt that Grandison, with the native
gregariousness and garrulousness of his race,
would foregather and palaver with them
sooner or later, and Dick hoped that they
would speedily inoculate him with the virus of
freedom. For it was not Dick's intention to
say anything to his servant about his plan to
free him, for obvious reasons. To mention
one of them, if Grandison should go away,
and by legal process be recaptured, his young
master's part in the matter would doubtless
become known, which would be embarrassing to Dick, to say the least. If, on the
other hand, he should merely give Grandison
sufficient latitude, he had no doubt he would
eventually lose him. For while not exactly
skeptical about Grandison's perfervid loyalty,
Dick had been a somewhat keen observer of
human nature, in his own indolent way, and
based his expectations upon the force of the
example and argument that his servant could
scarcely fail to encounter. Grandison should
have a fair chance to become free by his own
initiative ; if it should become necessary to

adopt other measures to get rid of him, it would be time enough to act when the necessity arose; and Dick Owens was not the youth to take needless trouble.

The young master renewed some acquaintances and made others, and spent a week or two very pleasantly in the best society of the metropolis, easily accessible to a wealthy, well-bred young Southerner, with proper introductions. Young women smiled on him, and young men of convivial habits pressed their hospitalities; but the memory of Charity's sweet, strong face and clear blue eyes made him proof against the blandishments of the one sex and the persuasions of the other. Meanwhile he kept Grandison supplied with pocket-money, and left him mainly to his own devices. Every night when Dick came in he hoped he might have to wait upon himself, and every morning he looked forward with pleasure to the prospect of making his toilet unaided. His hopes, however, were doomed to disappointment, for every night when he came in Grandison was on hand with a bootjack, and a nightcap mixed for his young master as the colonel had taught him to mix it, and every morning Grandison appeared with his master's boots blacked and his clothes brushed, and laid his linen out for the day.

" Grandison," said Dick one morning, after finishing his toilet, " this is the chance of your life to go around among your own people and see how they live. Have you met any of them ? "

" Yas, suh, I 's seen some of 'em. But I don' keer nuffin fer 'em, suh. Dey 're diffe'nt f'm de niggers down ou' way. Dey 'lows dey 're free, but dey ain' got sense 'nuff ter know dey ain' half as well off as dey would be down Souf, whar dey 'd be 'preciated."

When two weeks had passed without any apparent effect of evil example upon Grandison, Dick resolved to go on to Boston, where he thought the atmosphere might prove more favorable to his ends. After he had been at the Revere House for a day or two without losing Grandison, he decided upon slightly different tactics.

Having ascertained from a city directory the addresses of several well-known abolitionists, he wrote them each a letter something like this : —

DEAR FRIEND AND BROTHER: —

A wicked slaveholder from Kentucky, stopping at the Revere House, has dared to insult the liberty-loving people of Boston by bringing his slave into their midst. Shall this be tolerated? Or shall steps be taken in the name of liberty to rescue a fellow-man from bondage? For obvious reasons I can only sign myself,

A FRIEND OF HUMANITY.

That his letter might have an opportunity to prove effective, Dick made it a point to send Grandison away from the hotel on various errands. On one of these occasions Dick watched him for quite a distance down the street. Grandison had scarcely left the hotel when a long-haired, sharp-featured man came out behind him, followed him, soon overtook him, and kept along beside him until they turned the next corner. Dick's hopes were roused by this spectacle, but sank correspondingly when Grandison returned to the hotel. As Grandison said nothing about the encounter, Dick hoped there might be some self-consciousness behind this unexpected reticence, the results of which might develop later on.

But Grandison was on hand again when his master came back to the hotel at night, and was in attendance again in the morning, with hot water, to assist at his master's toilet. Dick sent him on further errands from day to day, and upon one occasion came squarely up to him — inadvertently of course — while Grandison was engaged in conversation with a young white man in clerical garb. When Grandison saw Dick approaching, he edged away from the preacher and hastened toward his master, with a very evident expression of relief upon his countenance.

" Mars Dick," he said, " dese yer abolitioners is jes' pesterin' de life out er me tryin' ter git me ter run away. I don' pay no 'tention ter 'em, but dey riles me so sometimes dat I 'm feared I 'll hit some of 'em some er dese days, an' dat mought git me inter trouble. I ain' said nuffin' ter you 'bout it, Mars Dick, fer I did n' wanter 'sturb yo' min'; but I don' like it, suh; no, suh, I don' ! Is we gwine back home 'fo' long, Mars Dick ? "

" We 'll be going back soon enough," replied Dick somewhat shortly, while he inwardly cursed the stupidity of a slave who could be free and would not, and registered

a secret vow that if he were unable to get rid
of Grandison without assassinating him, and
were therefore compelled to take him back to
Kentucky, he would see that Grandison got a
taste of an article of slavery that would make
him regret his wasted opportunities.   Meanwhile he determined to tempt his servant yet
more strongly.

"Grandison," he said next morning, "I'm
going away for a day or two, but I shall leave
you here.   I shall lock up a hundred dollars
in this drawer and give you the key.   If you
need any of it, use it and enjoy yourself, —
spend it all if you like, — for this is probably
the last chance you'll have for some time to
be in a free State, and you'd better enjoy
your liberty while you may."

When he came back a couple of days later
and found the faithful Grandison at his post,
and the hundred dollars intact, Dick felt seriously annoyed.   His vexation was increased
by the fact that he could not express his
feelings adequately.   He did not even scold
Grandison ; how could he, indeed, find fault
with one who so sensibly recognized his true
place in the economy of civilization, and kept
it with such touching fidelity ?

" I can't say a thing to him," groaned
Dick. " He deserves a leather medal, made
out of his own hide tanned. I reckon I 'll
write to father and let him know what a
model servant he has given me."

He wrote his father a letter which made the
colonel swell with pride and pleasure. " I
really think," the colonel observed to one of
his friends, " that Dick ought to have the
nigger interviewed by the Boston papers, so
that they may see how contented and happy
our darkeys really are."

Dick also wrote a long letter to Charity
Lomax, in which he said, among many other
things, that if she knew how hard he was
working, and under what difficulties, to accomplish something serious for her sake, she
would no longer keep him in suspense, but
overwhelm him with love and admiration.

Having thus exhausted without result the
more obvious methods of getting rid of Grandison, and diplomacy having also proved a
failure, Dick was forced to consider more
radical measures. Of course he might run
away himself, and abandon Grandison, but
this would be merely to leave him in the
United States, where he was still a slave, and

where, with his notions of loyalty, he would speedily be reclaimed. It was necessary, in order to accomplish the purpose of his trip to the North, to leave Grandison permanently in Canada, where he would be legally free.

"I might extend my trip to Canada," he reflected, "but that would be too palpable. I have it! I'll visit Niagara Falls on the way home, and lose him on the Canada side. When he once realizes that he is actually free, I'll warrant that he'll stay."

So the next day saw them westward bound, and in due course of time, by the somewhat slow conveyances of the period, they found themselves at Niagara. Dick walked and drove about the Falls for several days, taking Grandison along with him on most occasions. One morning they stood on the Canadian side, watching the wild whirl of the waters below them.

"Grandison," said Dick, raising his voice above the roar of the cataract, "do you know where you are now?"

"I's wid you, Mars Dick; dat's all I keers."

"You are now in Canada, Grandison, where your people go when they run away from their masters. If you wished, Grandison, you might walk away from me this very minute, and I could not lay my hand upon you to take you back."

Grandison looked around uneasily.

" Let's go back ober de ribber, Mars Dick. I's feared I'll lose you ovuh heah, an' den I won' hab no marster, an' won't nebber be able to git back home no mo'."

Discouraged, but not yet hopeless, Dick said, a few minutes later, —

" Grandison, I'm going up the road a bit, to the inn over yonder. You stay here until I return. I'll not be gone a great while."

Grandison's eyes opened wide and he looked somewhat fearful.

" Is dey any er dem dadblasted abolitioners roun' heah, Mars Dick ? "

" I don't imagine that there are," replied his master, hoping there might be. " But I'm not afraid of *your* running away, Grandison. I only wish I were," he added to himself.

Dick walked leisurely down the road to where the whitewashed inn, built of stone, with true British solidity, loomed up through the trees by the roadside. Arrived there he ordered a glass of ale and a sandwich, and took a seat at a table by a window, from which he could see Grandison in the distance. For a while he hoped that the seed he had sown might have fallen on fertile ground, and that Grandison, relieved from the restraining power of a master's eye, and finding himself in a free country, might get up and walk away; but the hope was vain, for Grandison remained faithfully at his post, awaiting his master's return. He had seated himself on a broad flat stone, and, turning his eyes away from the grand and awe-inspiring spectacle that lay close at hand, was looking anxiously toward the inn where his master sat cursing his ill-timed fidelity.

By and by a girl came into the room to serve his order, and Dick very naturally glanced at her; and as she was young and pretty and remained in attendance, it was some minutes before he looked for Grandison. When he did so his faithful servant had disappeared.

To pay his reckoning and go away without the change was a matter quickly accomplished. Retracing his footsteps toward the Falls, he saw, to his great disgust, as he approached the spot where he had left Grandison, the familiar form of his servant stretched out on the ground, his face to the sun, his mouth open, sleeping the time away, oblivious alike to the grandeur of the scenery, the thunderous roar of the cataract, or the insidious voice of sentiment.

"Grandison," soliloquized his master, as he stood gazing down at his ebony encumbrance, "I do not deserve to be an American citizen; I ought not to have the advantages I possess over you; and I certainly am not worthy of Charity Lomax, if I am not smart enough to get rid of you. I have an idea! You shall yet be free, and I will be the instrument of your deliverance. Sleep on, faithful and affectionate servitor, and dream of the blue grass and the bright skies of old Kentucky, for it is only in your dreams that you will ever see them again!"

Dick retraced his footsteps towards the inn. The young woman chanced to look out of the window and saw the handsome young gentleman she had waited on a few minutes before, standing in the road a short distance away, apparently engaged in earnest conversation with a colored man employed as hostler

for the inn.   She thought she saw something
pass from the white man to the other, but at
that moment her duties called her away from
the window, and when she looked out again
the young gentleman had disappeared, and
the hostler, with two other young men of the
neighborhood, one white and one colored,
were walking rapidly towards the Falls.

IV

Dick made the journey homeward alone,
and as rapidly as the conveyances of the day
would permit.   As he drew near home his
conduct in going back without Grandison
took on a more serious aspect than it had
borne at any previous time, and although he
had prepared the colonel by a letter sent
several days ahead, there was still the prospect of a bad quarter of an hour with him ;
not, indeed, that his father would upbraid
him, but he was likely to make searching inquiries.   And notwithstanding the vein of
quiet recklessness that had carried Dick
through his preposterous scheme, he was a
very poor liar, having rarely had occasion or
inclination to tell anything but the truth.

Any reluctance to meet his father was more than offset, however, by a stronger force drawing him homeward, for Charity Lomax must long since have returned from her visit to her aunt in Tennessee.

Dick got off easier than he had expected. He told a straight story, and a truthful one, so far as it went.

The colonel raged at first, but rage soon subsided into anger, and anger moderated into annoyance, and annoyance into a sort of garrulous sense of injury. The colonel thought he had been hardly used; he had trusted this negro, and he had broken faith. Yet, after all, he did not blame Grandison so much as he did the abolitionists, who were undoubtedly at the bottom of it.

As for Charity Lomax, Dick told her, privately of course, that he had run his father's man, Grandison, off to Canada, and left him there.

" Oh, Dick," she had said with shuddering alarm, " what have you done ? If they knew it they'd send you to the penitentiary, like they did that Yankee."

" But they don't know it," he had replied seriously; adding, with an injured tone, " you

don't seem to appreciate my heroism like
you did that of the Yankee; perhaps it's
because I was n't caught and sent to the
penitentiary. I thought you wanted me to
do it."

"Why, Dick Owens!" she exclaimed.
"You know I never dreamed of any such
outrageous proceeding.

"But I presume I'll have to marry you,"
she concluded, after some insistence on Dick's
part, "if only to take care of you. You
are too reckless for anything; and a man
who goes chasing all over the North, being
entertained by New York and Boston society
and having negroes to throw away, needs
some one to look after him."

"It's a most remarkable thing," replied
Dick fervently, "that your views correspond
exactly with my profoundest convictions. It
proves beyond question that we were made
for one another."

They were married three weeks later. As
each of them had just returned from a journey, they spent their honeymoon at home.

A week after the wedding they were seated,
one afternoon, on the piazza of the colonel's

house, where Dick had taken his bride, when
a negro from the yard ran down the lane and
threw open the big gate for the colonel's
buggy to enter. The colonel was not alone.
Beside him, ragged and travel-stained, bowed
with weariness, and upon his face a haggard
look that told of hardship and privation, sat
the lost Grandison.

The colonel alighted at the steps.

"Take the lines, Tom," he said to the
man who had opened the gate, "and drive
round to the barn. Help Grandison down, —
poor devil, he's so stiff he can hardly move!
— and get a tub of water and wash him and
rub him down, and feed him, and give him
a big drink of whiskey, and then let him
come round and see his young master and his
new mistress."

The colonel's face wore an expression com-
pounded of joy and indignation, — joy at
the restoration of a valuable piece of property; indignation for reasons he proceeded
to state.

"It's astounding, the depths of depravity
the human heart is capable of! I was coming along the road three miles away, when
I heard some one call me from the roadside.

I pulled up the mare, and who should come
out of the woods but Grandison. The poor
nigger could hardly crawl along, with the
help of a broken limb. I was never more
astonished in my life. You could have
knocked me down with a feather. He
seemed pretty far gone, — he could hardly
talk above a whisper, — and I had to give him
a mouthful of whiskey to brace him up so he
could tell his story. It's just as I thought
from the beginning, Dick ; Grandison had no
notion of running away ; he knew when he was
well off, and where his friends were. All the
persuasions of abolition liars and runaway
niggers did not move him. But the desper-
ation of those fanatics knew no bounds ;
their guilty consciences gave them no rest.
They got the notion somehow that Grandison
belonged to a nigger-catcher, and had been
brought North as a spy to help capture ungrateful runaway servants. They actually
kidnaped him — just think of it ! — and
gagged him and bound him and threw him
rudely into a wagon, and carried him into
the gloomy depths of a Canadian forest, and
locked him in a lonely hut, and fed him on
bread and water for three weeks. One of the

scoundrels wanted to kill him, and persuaded the others that it ought to be done ; but they got to quarreling about how they should do it, and before they had their minds made up Grandison escaped, and, keeping his back steadily to the North Star, made his way, after suffering incredible hardships, back to the old plantation, back to his master, his friends, and his home. Why, it's as good as one of Scott's novels! Mr. Simms or some other one of our Southern authors ought to write it up."

"Don't you think, sir," suggested Dick, who had calmly smoked his cigar throughout the colonel's animated recital, "that that kidnaping yarn sounds a little improbable ? Is n't there some more likely explanation ?"

"Nonsense, Dick; it's the gospel truth! Those infernal abolitionists are capable of anything — everything! Just think of their locking the poor, faithful nigger up, beating him, kicking him, depriving him of his liberty, keeping him on bread and water for three long, lonesome weeks, and he all the time pining for the old plantation !"

There were almost tears in the colonel's eyes at the picture of Grandison's sufferings

that he conjured up. Dick still professed
to be slightly skeptical, and met Charity's
severely questioning eye with bland unconsciousness.

The colonel killed the fatted calf for
Grandison, and for two or three weeks the
returned wanderer's life was a slave's dream
of pleasure. His fame spread throughout
the county, and the colonel gave him a permanent place among the house servants,
where he could always have him conveniently
at hand to relate his adventures to admiring
visitors.

About three weeks after Grandison's return
the colonel's faith in sable humanity was
rudely shaken, and its foundations almost
broken up. He came near losing his belief
in the fidelity of the negro to his master, —
the servile virtue most highly prized and
most sedulously cultivated by the colonel and
his kind. One Monday morning Grandison
was missing. And not only Grandison, but
his wife, Betty the maid ; his mother, aunt
Eunice ; his father, uncle Ike ; his brothers,
Tom and John, and his little sister Elsie,
were likewise absent from the plantation ;

and a hurried search and inquiry in the
neighborhood resulted in no information as
to their whereabouts. So much valuable
property could not be lost without an effort
to recover it, and the wholesale nature of the
transaction carried consternation to the hearts
of those whose ledgers were chiefly bound in
black. Extremely energetic measures were
taken by the colonel and his friends. The
fugitives were traced, and followed from point
to point, on their northward run through
Ohio. Several times the hunters were close
upon their heels, but the magnitude of the
escaping party begot unusual vigilance on
the part of those who sympathized with the
fugitives, and strangely enough, the under-
ground railroad seemed to have had its tracks
cleared and signals set for this particular
train. Once, twice, the colonel thought he
had them, but they slipped through his
fingers.

One last glimpse he caught of his vanishing
property, as he stood, accompanied by a United
States marshal, on a wharf at a port on the
south shore of Lake Erie. On the stern of a
small steamboat which was receding rapidly
from the wharf, with her nose pointing toward

Canada, there stood a group of familiar dark faces, and the look they cast backward was not one of longing for the fleshpots of Egypt. The colonel saw Grandison point him out to one of the crew of the vessel, who waved his hand derisively toward the colonel. The latter shook his fist impotently — and the incident was closed.

UNCLE WELLINGTON'S WIVES

I

UNCLE WELLINGTON BRABOY was so deeply absorbed in thought as he walked slowly homeward from the weekly meeting of the Union League, that he let his pipe go out, a fact of which he remained oblivious until he had reached the little frame house in the suburbs of Patesville, where he lived with aunt Milly, his wife. On this particular occasion the club had been addressed by a visiting brother from the North, Professor Patterson, a tall, well-formed mulatto, who wore a perfectly fitting suit of broadcloth, a shiny silk hat, and linen of dazzling whiteness, —in short, a gentleman of such distinguished appearance that the doors and windows of the offices and stores on Front Street were filled with curious observers as he passed through that thoroughfare in the early part of the day. This polished stranger was a traveling organizer of Masonic lodges, but he also

claimed to be a high officer in the Union
League, and had been invited to lecture be-
fore the local chapter of that organization at
Patesville.

The lecture had been largely attended, and
uncle Wellington Braboy had occupied a seat
just in front of the platform. The subject of
the lecture was " The Mental, Moral, Physical,
Political, Social, and Financial Improvement
of the Negro Race in America," a theme much
dwelt upon, with slight variations, by colored
orators. For to this struggling people, then
as now, the problem of their uncertain present
and their doubtful future was the chief concern of life. The period was the hopeful
one. The Federal Government retained
some vestige of authority in the South, and
the newly emancipated race cherished the
delusion that under the Constitution, that
enduring rock on which our liberties are
founded, and under the equal laws it pur-
ported to guarantee, they would enter upon
the era of freedom and opportunity which
their Northern friends had inaugurated with
such solemn sanctions. The speaker pictured
in eloquent language the state of ideal equality and happiness enjoyed by colored people

at the North : how they sent their children
to school with the white children ; how they
sat by white people in the churches and thea-
tres, ate with them in the public restaurants,
and buried their dead in the same cemeteries.
The professor waxed eloquent with the development of his theme, and, as a finishing
touch to an alluring picture, assured the excited audience that the intermarriage of the
races was common, and that he himself had
espoused a white woman.

Uncle Wellington Braboy was a deeply interested listener. He had heard something
of these facts before, but his information had
always come in such vague and questionable
shape that he had paid little attention to it.
He knew that the Yankees had freed the
slaves, and that runaway negroes had always
gone to the North to seek liberty ; any such
equality, however, as the visiting brother had
depicted, was more than uncle Wellington
had ever conceived as actually existing anywhere in the world. At first he felt inclined
to doubt the truth of the speaker's statements ;
but the cut of his clothes, the eloquence of
his language, and the flowing length of his
whiskers, were so far superior to anything

uncle Wellington had ever met among the
colored people of his native State, that he felt
irresistibly impelled to the conviction that nothing less than the advantages claimed for the
North by the visiting brother could have produced such an exquisite flower of civilization.
Any lingering doubts uncle Wellington may
have felt were entirely dispelled by the courtly
bow and cordial grasp of the hand with which
the visiting brother acknowledged the con-
gratulations showered upon him by the audience at the close of his address.

The more uncle Wellington's mind dwelt
upon the professor's speech, the more attractive seemed the picture of Northern life presented. Uncle Wellington possessed in large
measure the imaginative faculty so freely bestowed by nature upon the race from which
the darker half of his blood was drawn. He
had indulged in occasional day-dreams of an
ideal state of social equality, but his wildest
flights of fancy had never located it nearer
than heaven, and he had felt some misgivings
about its practical working even there. Its
desirability he had never doubted, and the
speech of the evening before had given a
local habitation and a name to the forms his

imagination had bodied forth. Giving full
rein to his fancy, he saw in the North a land
flowing with milk and honey, — a land peo-
pled by noble men and beautiful women,
among whom colored men and women moved
with the ease and grace of acknowledged
right. Then he placed himself in the fore-
ground of the picture. What a fine figure he
would have made in the world if he had been
born at the free North! He imagined himself dressed like the professor, and passing
the contribution-box in a white church; and
most pleasant of his dreams, and the hardest
to realize as possible, was that of the gracious
white lady he might have called wife. Uncle
Wellington was a mulatto, and his features
were those of his white father, though tinged
with the hue of his mother's race; and as
he lifted the kerosene lamp at evening, and
took a long look at his image in the little
mirror over the mantelpiece, he said to himself that he was a very good-looking man,
and could have adorned a much higher sphere
in life than that in which the accident of
birth had placed him. He fell asleep and
dreamed that he lived in a two-story brick
house, with a spacious flower garden in front,

the whole inclosed by a high iron fence; that
he kept a carriage and servants, and never did
a stroke of work. This was the highest style
of living in Patesville, and he could conceive
of nothing finer.

Uncle Wellington slept later than usual the
next morning, and the sunlight was pouring
in at the open window of the bedroom, when
his dreams were interrupted by the voice of
his wife, in tones meant to be harsh, but
which no ordinary degree of passion could
rob of their native unctuousness.

"Git up f'm dere, you lazy, good-fuh-nuf-
fin' nigger! Is you gwine ter sleep all de
mawnin'?   I's ti'ed er dis yer runnin' 'roun'
all night an' den sleepin' all day. You won't
git dat tater patch hoed ovuh ter-day 'less'n
you git up f'm dere an' git at it."

Uncle Wellington rolled over, yawned cav-
ernously, stretched himself, and with a muttered protest got out of bed and put on his
clothes. Aunt Milly had prepared a smoking
breakfast of hominy and fried bacon, the odor
of which was very grateful to his nostrils.

"Is breakfus' done ready?" he inquired,
tentatively, as he came into the kitchen and
glanced at the table.

" No, it ain't ready, an' 't ain't gwine ter be
ready 'tel you tote dat wood an' water in," replied aunt Milly severely, as she poured two
teacups of boiling water on two tablespoon-
fuls of ground coffee.

Uncle Wellington went down to the spring
and got a pail of water, after which he
brought in some oak logs for the fireplace
and some lightwood for kindling. Then he
drew a chair towards the table and started to
sit down.

" Wonduh what 's de matter wid you dis
mawnin' anyhow," remarked aunt Milly.
" You must 'a' be'n up ter some devilment
las' night, fer yo' recommemb'ance is so po'
dat you fus' fergit ter git up, an' den fergit
ter wash yo' face an' hands fo' you set down
ter de table. I don' 'low nobody ter eat at
my table dat a-way."

" I don' see no use 'n washin' 'em so
much," replied Wellington wearily. " Dey
gits dirty ag'in right off, an' den you got ter
wash 'em ovuh ag'in ; it 's jes' pilin' up wuk
what don' fetch in nuffin'. De dirt don'
show nohow, 'n' I don' see no advantage in
bein' black, ef you got to keep on washin'
yo' face 'n' han's jes' lack w'ite folks." He

nevertheless performed his ablutions in a perfunctory way, and resumed his seat at the breakfast-table.

"Ole 'oman," he asked, after the edge of his appetite had been taken off, "how would you lack ter live at de Norf?"

"I dunno nuffin' 'bout de Norf," replied aunt Milly. "It's hard 'nuff ter git erlong heah, whar we knows all erbout it."

"De brother what 'dressed de meetin' las' night say dat de wages at de Norf is twicet ez big ez dey is heah."

"You could make a sight mo' wages heah ef you 'd 'ten' ter yo' wuk better," replied aunt Milly.

Uncle Wellington ignored this personality, and continued, "An' he say de cullud folks got all de privileges er de w'ite folks, — dat dey chillen goes ter school tergedder, dat dey sets on same seats in chu'ch, an' sarves on jury, 'n' rides on de kyars an' steamboats wid de w'ite folks, an' eats at de fus' table."

"Dat 'u'd suit you," chuckled aunt Milly, "an' you 'd stay dere fer de secon' table, too. How dis man know 'bout all dis yer foolis'-ness?" she asked incredulously.

"He come f'm de Norf," said uncle Wellington, "an' he 'speunced it all hisse'f."

"Well, he can't make me b'lieve it," she rejoined, with a shake of her head.

"An' you would n' lack ter go up dere an' 'joy all dese privileges?" asked uncle Wellington, with some degree of earnestness.

The old woman laughed until her sides shook. "Who gwine ter take me up dere?" she inquired.

"You got de money yo'se'f."

"I ain' got no money fer ter was'e," she replied shortly, becoming serious at once; and with that the subject was dropped.

Uncle Wellington pulled a hoe from under the house, and took his way wearily to the potato patch. He did not feel like working, but aunt Milly was the undisputed head of the establishment, and he did not dare to openly neglect his work. In fact, he regarded work at any time as a disagreeable necessity to be avoided as much as possible.

His wife was cast in a different mould. Externally she would have impressed the casual observer as a neat, well-preserved, and good-looking black woman, of middle age, every curve of whose ample figure — and her figure was all curves — was suggestive of repose. So far from being indolent, or even deliberate in her movements, she was the most active and energetic woman in the town. She went through the physical exercises of a prayer-meeting with astonishing vigor. It was exhilarating to see her wash a shirt, and a study to watch her do it up. A quick jerk shook out the dampened garment; one pass of her ample palm spread it over the ironing-board, and a few well-directed strokes with the iron accomplished what would have occupied the ordinary laundress for half an hour.

To this uncommon, and in uncle Wellington's opinion unnecessary and unnatural activity, his own habits were a steady protest. If aunt Milly had been willing to support him in idleness, he would have acquiesced without a murmur in her habits of industry. This she would not do, and, moreover, insisted on his working at least half the time. If she had invested the proceeds of her labor in rich food and fine clothing, he might have endured it better; but to her passion for work was added a most detestable thrift. She absolutely refused to pay for Wellington's clothes, and required him to furnish a certain proportion of the family supplies. Her savings were carefully put by, and with them she had bought and paid for the modest cottage which she and her husband occupied. Under her careful hand it was always neat and clean; in summer the little yard was gay with bright-colored flowers, and woe to the heedless pickaninny who should stray into her yard and pluck a rose or a verbena! In a stout oaken chest under her bed she kept a capacious stocking, into which flowed a steady stream of fractional currency. She carried the key to this chest in her pocket, a proceeding regarded by uncle Wellington with no little disfavor. He was of the opinion — an opinion he would not have dared to assert in her presence — that his wife's earnings were his own property; and he looked upon this stocking as a drunkard's wife might regard the saloon which absorbed her husband's wages.

Uncle Wellington hurried over the potato patch on the morning of the conversation above recorded, and as soon as he saw aunt

Milly go away with a basket of clothes on
her head, returned to the house, put on his
coat, and went uptown.

He directed his steps to a small frame
building fronting on the main street of the
village, at a point where the street was inter-
sected by one of the several creeks mean-
dering through the town, cooling the air,
providing numerous swimming-holes for the
amphibious small boy, and furnishing water-
power for grist-mills and saw-mills. The rear
of the building rested on long brick pillars,
built up from the bottom of the steep bank
of the creek, while the front was level with
the street. This was the office of Mr. Mat-
thew Wright, the sole representative of the
colored race at the bar of Chinquapin County.
Mr. Wright came of an "old issue" free
colored family, in which, though the negro
blood was present in an attenuated strain, a
line of free ancestry could be traced beyond
the Revolutionary War. He had enjoyed
exceptional opportunities, and enjoyed the
distinction of being the first, and for a long
time the only colored lawyer in North Carolina. His services were frequently called into
requisition by impecunious people of his own

race; when they had money they went to white lawyers, who, they shrewdly conjectured, would have more influence with judge or jury than a colored lawyer, however able.

Uncle Wellington found Mr. Wright in his office. Having inquired after the health of the lawyer's family and all his relations in detail, uncle Wellington asked for a professional opinion.

"Mistah Wright, ef a man's wife got money, whose money is dat befo' de law — his'n er her'n ? "

The lawyer put on his professional air, and replied : —

" Under the common law, which in default of special legislative enactment is the law of North Carolina, the personal property of the wife belongs to her husband."

"But dat don' jes' tech de p'int, suh. I wuz axin' 'bout money."

" You see, uncle Wellington, your education has not rendered you familiar with legal phraseology. The term ' personal property ' or ' estate ' embraces, according to Blackstone, all property other than land, and therefore includes money. ˙Any money a man's wife has is his, constructively, and will be recognized as his actually, as soon as he can secure possession of it."

"Dat is ter say, suh — my eddication don' quite 'low me ter understan' dat — dat is ter say " —

"That is to say, it 's yours when you get it. It is n't yours so that the law will help you get it; but on the other hand, when you once lay your hands on it, it is yours so that the law won't take it away from you."

Uncle Wellington nodded to express his full comprehension of the law as expounded by Mr. Wright, but scratched his head in a way that expressed some disappointment. The law seemed to wobble. Instead of enabling him to stand up fearlessly and demand his own, it threw him back upon his own efforts; and the prospect of his being able to overpower or outwit aunt Milly by any ordinary means was very poor.

He did not leave the office, but hung around awhile as though there were something further he wished to speak about. Finally, after some discursive remarks about the crops and politics, he asked, in an offhand, disinterested manner, as though the thought had just occurred to him : —

" Mistah Wright, w'ile 's we 're talkin' 'bout law matters, what do it cos' ter git a defoce ? "

" That depends upon circumstances. It is n't altogether a matter of expense. Have you and aunt Milly been having trouble ? "

" Oh no, suh ; I was jes' a-wond'rin'."

" You see," continued the lawyer, who was fond of talking, and had nothing else to do for the moment, " a divorce is not an easy thing to get in this State under any circumstances. It used to be the law that divorce could be granted only by special act of the legislature ; and it is but recently that the subject has been relegated to the jurisdiction of the courts."

Uncle Wellington understood a part of this, but the answer had not been exactly to the point in his mind.

" S'pos'n', den, jes' fer de argyment, me an' my ole 'oman sh'd fall out en wanter separate, how could I git a defoce ? "

" That would depend on what you quarreled about. It 's pretty hard work to answer general questions in a particular way. If you merely wished to separate, it would n't be necessary to get a divorce ; but if you should want to marry again, you would have to be

divorced, or else you would be guilty of
bigamy, and could be sent to the penitentiary.
But, by the way, uncle Wellington, when
were you married ? "

" I got married 'fo' de wah, when I was
livin' down on Rockfish Creek."

" When you were in slavery ? "

" Yas, suh."

" Did you have your marriage registered
after the surrender ? "

" No, suh ; never knowed nuffin' 'bout dat."

After the war, in North Carolina and other
States, the freed people who had sustained
to each other the relation of husband and
wife as it existed among slaves, were required
by law to register their consent to continue
in the marriage relation.   By this simple expedient their former marriages of convenience
received the sanction of law, and their children the seal of legitimacy.   In many cases,
however, where the parties lived in districts
remote from the larger towns, the ceremony
was neglected, or never heard of by the
freedmen.

" Well," said the lawyer, " if that is the case,
and you and aunt Milly should disagree, it
wouldn't be necessary for you to get a divorce,

even if you should want to marry again. You were never legally married."

" So Milly ain't my lawful wife, den ? "

"She may be your wife in one sense of the word, but not in such a sense as to render you liable to punishment for bigamy if you should marry another woman. But I hope you will never want to do anything of the kind, for you have a very good wife now."

Uncle Wellington went away thoughtfully, but with a feeling of unaccustomed lightness and freedom. He had not felt so free since the memorable day when he had first heard of the Emancipation Proclamation. On leaving the lawyer's office, he called at the workshop of one of his friends, Peter Williams, a shoemaker by trade, who had a brother living in Ohio.

" Is you hearn f'm Sam lately ? " uncle Wellington inquired, after the conversation had drifted through the usual generalities.

"His mammy got er letter f'm 'im las' week; he 's livin' in de town er Groveland now."

" How 's he gittin' on ? "

" He says he gittin' on monst'us well. He 'low ez how he make five dollars a day w'ite-washin', an' have all he kin do."

The shoemaker related various details of his brother's prosperity, and uncle Wellington returned home in a very thoughtful mood, revolving in his mind a plan of future action. This plan had been vaguely assuming form ever since the professor's lecture, and the events of the morning had brought out the detail in bold relief.

Two days after the conversation with the shoemaker, aunt Milly went, in the afternoon, to visit a sister of hers who lived several miles out in the country. During her absence, which lasted until nightfall, uncle Wellington went uptown and purchased a cheap oil-cloth valise from a shrewd son of Israel, who had penetrated to this locality with a stock of notions and cheap clothing. Uncle Wellington had his purchase done up in brown paper, and took the parcel under his arm. Arrived at home he unwrapped the valise, and thrust into its capacious jaws his best suit of clothes, some underwear, and a few other small articles for personal use and adornment. Then he carried the valise out into the yard, and, first looking cautiously around to see if there was any one in sight, concealed it in a clump of bushes in a corner of the yard.

It may be inferred from this proceeding that uncle Wellington was preparing for a step of some consequence. In fact, he had fully made up his mind to go to the North; but he still lacked the most important requisite for traveling with comfort, namely, the money to pay his expenses. The idea of tramping the distance which separated him from the promised land of liberty and equality had never occurred to him. When a slave, he had several times been importuned by fellow servants to join them in the attempt to escape from bondage, but he had never wanted his freedom badly enough to walk a thousand miles for it; if he could have gone to Canada by stage-coach, or by rail, or on horseback, with stops for regular meals, he would probably have undertaken the trip. The funds he now needed for his journey were in aunt Milly's chest. He had thought a great deal about his right to this money. It was his wife's savings, and he had never dared to dispute, openly, her right to exercise exclusive control over what she earned; but the lawyer had assured him of his right to the money, of which he was already constructively in possession, and he had therefore deter-

mined to possess himself actually of the
coveted stocking. It was impracticable for
him to get the key of the chest. Aunt Milly
kept it in her pocket by day and under her
pillow at night. She was a light sleeper, and,
if not awakened by the abstraction of the
key, would certainly have been disturbed by
the unlocking of the chest. But one alterna-
tive remained, and that was to break open the
chest in her absence.

There was a revival in progress at the colored Methodist church. Aunt Milly was as
energetic in her religion as in other respects,
and had not missed a single one of the meetings. She returned at nightfall from her
visit to the country and prepared a frugal
supper. Uncle Wellington did not eat as
heartily as usual. Aunt Milly perceived his
want of appetite, and spoke of it. He explained it by saying that he did not feel very
well.

" Is you gwine ter chu'ch ter-night ? "
inquired his wife.

" I reckon I 'll stay home an' go ter bed,"
he replied. " I ain't be'n feelin' well dis
evenin', an' I 'spec' I better git a good night's
res'."

" Well, you kin stay ef you mineter. Good
preachin' 'u'd make you feel better, but ef
you ain't gwine, don' fergit ter tote in some
wood an' lighterd 'fo' you go ter bed. De
moon is shinin' bright, an' you can't have no
'scuse 'bout not bein' able ter see."

Uncle Wellington followed her out to the
gate, and watched her receding form until it
disappeared in the distance. Then he re-
entered the house with a quick step, and taking a hatchet from a corner of the room, drew
the chest from under the bed. As he applied
the hatchet to the fastenings, a thought
struck him, and by the flickering light of the
pine-knot blazing on the hearth, a look of
hesitation might have been seen to take the
place of the determined expression his face
had worn up to that time. He had argued
himself into the belief that his present action
was lawful and justifiable. Though this conviction had not prevented him from trembling
in every limb, as though he were committing
a mere vulgar theft, it had still nerved him to
the deed. Now even his moral courage began
to weaken. The lawyer had told him that his
wife's property was his own; in taking it he
was therefore only exercising his lawful right.

But at the point of breaking open the chest, it occurred to him that he was taking this money in order to get away from aunt Milly, and that he justified his desertion of her by the lawyer's opinion that she was not his lawful wife. If she was not his wife, then he had no right to take the money; if she was his wife, he had no right to desert her, and would certainly have no right to marry another woman. His scheme was about to go to shipwreck on this rock, when another idea occurred to him.

"De lawyer say dat in one sense er de word de ole 'oman is my wife, an' in anudder sense er de word she ain't my wife. Ef I goes ter de Norf an' marry a w'ite 'oman, I ain't commit no brigamy, 'caze in dat sense er de word she ain't my wife; but ef I takes dis money, I ain't stealin' it, 'caze in dat sense er de word she is my wife. Dat 'splains all de trouble away."

Having reached this ingenious conclusion, uncle Wellington applied the hatchet vigorously, soon loosened the fastenings of the chest, and with trembling hands extracted from its depths a capacious blue cotton stocking. He emptied the stocking on the table.

His first impulse was to take the whole, but again there arose in his mind a doubt — a very obtrusive, unreasonable doubt, but a doubt, nevertheless — of the absolute rectitude of his conduct ; and after a moment's hesitation he hurriedly counted the money — it was in bills of small denominations — and found it to be about two hundred and fifty dollars. He then divided it into two piles of one hundred and twenty-five dollars each. He put one pile into his pocket, returned the remainder to the stocking, and replaced it where he had found it. He then closed the chest and shoved it under the bed. After having arranged the fire so that it could safely be left burning, he took a last look around the room, and went out into the moonlight, locking the door behind him, and hanging the key on a nail in the wall, where his wife would be likely to look for it. He then secured his valise from behind the bushes, and left the yard. As he passed by the wood-pile, he said to himself : —

" Well, I declar' ef I ain't done fergot ter tote in dat lighterd; I reckon de ole 'oman, 'll ha' ter fetch it in herse'f dis time."

He hastened through the quiet streets,

avoiding the few people who were abroad at that hour, and soon reached the railroad station, from which a North-bound train left at nine o'clock. He went around to the dark side of the train, and climbed into a second-class car, where he shrank into the darkest corner and turned his face away from the dim light of the single dirty lamp. There were no passengers in the car except one or two sleepy negroes, who had got on at some other station, and a white man who had gone into the car to smoke, accompanied by a gigantic bloodhound.

Finally the train crept out of the station. From the window uncle Wellington looked out upon the familiar cabins and turpentine stills, the new barrel factory, the brickyard where he had once worked for some time; and as the train rattled through the outskirts of the town, he saw gleaming in the moonlight the white headstones of the colored cemetery where his only daughter had been buried several years before.

Presently the conductor came around. Uncle Wellington had not bought a ticket, and the conductor collected a cash fare. He was not acquainted with uncle Wellington,

but had just had a drink at the saloon near
the depot, and felt at peace with all mankind.

" Where are you going, uncle? " he inquired carelessly.

Uncle Wellington's face assumed the ashen
hue which does duty for pallor in dusky
countenances, and his knees began to tremble.
Controlling his voice as well as he could, he
replied that he was going up to Jonesboro,
the terminus of the railroad, to work for a
gentleman at that place. He felt immensely
relieved when the conductor pocketed the
fare, picked up his lantern, and moved away.
It was very unphilosophical and very absurd
that a man who was only doing right should
feel like a thief, shrink from the sight of
other people, and lie instinctively. Fine distinctions were not in uncle Wellington's line,
but he was struck by the unreasonableness of
his feelings, and still more by the discomfort
they caused him. By and by, however, the
motion of the train made him drowsy; his
thoughts all ran together in confusion; and
he fell asleep with his head on his valise, and
one hand in his pocket, clasped tightly around
the roll of money.

II

The train from Pittsburg drew into the
Union Depot at Groveland, Ohio, one morning in the spring of 187–, with bell ringing
and engine puffing ; and from a smoking-car
emerged the form of uncle Wellington Braboy, a little dusty and travel-stained, and with
a sleepy look about his eyes. He mingled in
the crowd, and, valise in hand, moved toward
the main exit from the depot. There were
several tracks to be crossed, and more than
once a watchman snatched him out of the
way of a baggage-truck, or a train backing
into the depot. He at length reached the
door, beyond which, and as near as the regu-
lations would permit, stood a number of hack-
men, vociferously soliciting patronage. One
of them, a colored man, soon secured several
passengers. As he closed the door after the
last one he turned to uncle Wellington, who
stood near him on the sidewalk, looking about
irresolutely.

"Is you goin' uptown?" asked the hackman, as he prepared to mount the box.

" Yas, suh."

" I 'll take you up fo' a quahtah, ef you

want ter git up here an' ride on de box wid me."

Uncle Wellington accepted the offer and mounted the box. The hackman whipped up his horses, the carriage climbed the steep hill leading up to the town, and the passengers inside were soon deposited at their hotels.

" Whereabouts do you want to go ? " asked the hackman of uncle Wellington, when the carriage was emptied of its last passengers.

" I want ter go ter Brer Sam Williams's," said Wellington.

" What 's his street an' number ? "

Uncle Wellington did not know the street and number, and the hackman had to explain to him the mystery of numbered houses, to which he was a total stranger.

" Where is he from ? " asked the hackman, " and what is his business ? "

" He is f'm Norf Ca'lina," replied uncle Wellington, " an' makes his livin' w'ite-washin'."

" I reckon I knows de man," said the hackman. " I 'spec' he 's changed his name. De man I knows is name' Johnson. He b'longs ter my chu'ch. I 'm gwine out dat way ter git a passenger fer de ten o'clock train, an' I 'll take you by dere."

They followed one of the least handsome
streets of the city for more than a mile,
turned into a cross street, and drew up before
a small frame house, from the front of which
a sign, painted in white upon a black background, announced to the reading public, in
letters inclined to each other at various angles, that whitewashing and kalsomining were
" dun " there. A knock at the door brought
out a slatternly looking colored woman. She
had evidently been disturbed at her toilet, for
she held a comb in one hand, and the hair on
one side of her head stood out loosely, while
on the other side it was braided close to her
head. She called her husband, who proved
to be the Patesville shoemaker's brother.
The hackman introduced the traveler, whose
name he had learned on the way out, collected
his quarter, and drove away.

Mr. Johnson, the shoemaker's brother, welcomed uncle Wellington to Groveland, and
listened with eager delight to the news of the
old town, from which he himself had run
away many years before, and followed the
North Star to Groveland. He had changed
his name from " Williams " to " Johnson," on
account of the Fugitive Slave Law, which,

at the time of his escape from bondage, had rendered it advisable for runaway slaves to court obscurity. After the war he had retained the adopted name. Mrs. Johnson prepared breakfast for her guest, who ate it with an appetite sharpened by his journey. After breakfast he went to bed, and slept until late in the afternoon.

After supper Mr. Johnson took uncle Wellington to visit some of the neighbors who had come from North Carolina before the war. They all expressed much pleasure at meeting " Mr. Braboy," a title which at first sounded a little odd to uncle Wellington. At home he had been " Wellin'ton," " Brer Wellin'ton," or " uncle Wellin'ton ; " it was a novel experience to be called " Mister," and he set it down, with secret satisfaction, as one of the first fruits of Northern liberty.

" Would you lack ter look 'roun' de town a little ? " asked Mr. Johnson at breakfast next morning. " I ain' got no job dis mawnin', an' I kin show you some er de sights."

Uncle Wellington acquiesced in this arrangement, and they walked up to the corner to the street-car line. In a few moments a car passed. Mr. Johnson jumped on the

moving car, and uncle Wellington followed
his example, at the risk of life or limb, as it
was his first experience of street cars.

There was only one vacant seat in the car
and that was between two white women in
the forward end.   Mr. Johnson motioned to
the seat, but Wellington shrank from walking
between those two rows of white people, to
say nothing of sitting between the two women,
so he remained standing in the rear part of
the car.   A moment later, as the car rounded
a short curve, he was pitched sidewise into
the lap of a stout woman magnificently at-
tired in a ruffled blue calico gown.   The
lady colored up, and uncle Wellington, as he
struggled to his feet amid the laughter of the
passengers, was absolutely helpless with embarrassment, until the conductor came up
behind him and pushed him toward the
vacant place.

" Sit down, will you," he said ; and before
uncle Wellington could collect himself, he
was seated between the two white women.
Everybody in the car seemed to be looking at
him.   But he came to the conclusion, after
he had pulled himself together and reflected
a few moments, that he would find this

method of locomotion pleasanter when he
got used to it, and then he could score one
more glorious privilege gained by his change
of residence.

They got off at the public square, in the
heart of the city, where there were flowers
and statues, and fountains playing. Mr.
Johnson pointed out the court-house, the
post-office, the jail, and other public buildings fronting on the square. They visited the
market near by, and from an elevated point,
looked down upon the extensive lumber yards
and factories that were the chief sources of
the city's prosperity. Beyond these they could
see the fleet of ships that lined the coal
and iron ore docks of the harbor. Mr. Johnson, who was quite a fluent talker, enlarged
upon the wealth and prosperity of the city;
and Wellington, who had never before been
in a town of more than three thousand inhab-
itants, manifested sufficient interest and wonder to satisfy the most exacting *cicerone*.
They called at the office of a colored lawyer
and member of the legislature, formerly from
North Carolina, who, scenting a new constitu-
ent and a possible client, greeted the stranger
warmly, and in flowing speech pointed out

the superior advantages of life at the North,
citing himself as an illustration of the possi-
bilities of life in a country really free. As
they wended their way homeward to dinner
uncle Wellington, with quickened pulse and
rising hopes, felt that this was indeed the
promised land, and that it must be flowing
with milk and honey.

Uncle Wellington remained at the residence
of Mr. Johnson for several weeks before making any effort to find employment. He spent
this period in looking about the city. The
most commonplace things possessed for him
the charm of novelty, and he had come prepared to admire. Shortly after his arrival, he
had offered to pay for his board, intimating
at the same time that he had plenty of money.
Mr. Johnson declined to accept anything
from him for board, and expressed himself as
being only too proud to have Mr. Braboy remain in the house on the footing of an honored guest, until he had settled himself. He
lightened in some degree, however, the burden
of obligation under which a prolonged stay
on these terms would have placed his guest,
by soliciting from the latter occasional small
loans, until uncle Wellington's roll of money

began to lose its plumpness, and with an
empty pocket staring him in the face, he felt
the necessity of finding something to do.

During his residence in the city he had met
several times his first acquaintance, Mr. Peterson, the hackman, who from time to time
inquired how he was getting along. On one
of these occasions Wellington mentioned his
willingness to accept employment. As good
luck would have it, Mr. Peterson knew of
a vacant situation. He had formerly been
coachman for a wealthy gentleman residing
on Oakwood Avenue, but had resigned the
situation to go into business for himself. His
place had been filled by an Irishman, who
had just been discharged for drunkenness, and
the gentleman that very day had sent word to
Mr. Peterson, asking him if he could recom-
mend a competent and trustworthy coachman.

"Does you know anything erbout hosses?"
asked Mr. Peterson.

"Yas, indeed, I does," said Wellington.
"I wuz raise' 'mongs' hosses."

"I tol' my ole boss I 'd look out fer a man,
an' ef you reckon you kin fill de 'quirements
er de situation, I 'll take yo' roun' dere ter-
morrer mornin'. You wants ter put on yo'

bes' clothes an' slick up, fer dey 're partic'lar
people.   Ef you git de place I 'll expec' you
ter pay me fer de time I lose in 'tendin' ter
yo' business, fer time is money in dis country,
an' folks don't do much fer nuthin'."

Next morning Wellington blacked his shoes
carefully, put on a clean collar, and with the
aid of Mrs. Johnson tied his cravat in a
jaunty bow which gave him quite a sprightly
air and a much younger look than his years
warranted.   Mr. Peterson called for him at
eight o'clock.   After traversing several cross
streets they turned into Oakwood Avenue and
walked along the finest part of it for about
half a mile.   The handsome houses of this
famous avenue, the stately trees, the wide-
spreading lawns, dotted with flower beds,
fountains and statuary, made up a picture so
far surpassing anything in Wellington's experience as to fill him with an almost oppres-
sive sense of its beauty.

" Hit looks lack hebben," he said softly.

" It 's a pootty fine street," rejoined his
companion, with a judicial air, " but I don't
like dem big lawns.   It 's too much trouble
ter keep de grass down.   One er dem lawns
is big enough to pasture a couple er cows."

They went down a street running at right angles to the avenue, and turned into the rear of the corner lot. A large building of pressed brick, trimmed with stone, loomed up before them.

" Do de gemman lib in dis house ? " asked Wellington, gazing with awe at the front of the building.

" No, dat 's de barn," said Mr. Peterson with good-natured contempt ; and leading the way past a clump of shrubbery to the dwelling-house, he went up the back steps and rang the door-bell.

The ring was answered by a buxom Irish-woman, of a natural freshness of complexion deepened to a fiery red by the heat of a kitchen range. Wellington thought he had seen her before, but his mind had received so many new impressions lately that it was a minute or two before he recognized in her the lady whose lap he had involuntarily occupied for a moment on his first day in Groveland.

" Faith," she exclaimed as she admitted them, " an' it 's mighty glad I am to see ye ag'in, Misther Payterson ! An' how hev ye be'n, Misther Payterson, sence I see ye lahst ? "

" Middlin' well, Mis' Flannigan, middlin'
well, 'ceptin' a tech er de rheumatiz.   S'pose
you be'n doin' well as usual ? "

" Oh yis, as well as a dacent woman could
do wid a drunken baste about the place like
the lahst coachman.   O Misther Payterson,
it would make yer heart bleed to see the way
the spalpeen cut up a-Saturday ! But Misther
Todd discharged 'im the same avenin', widout
a characther, bad 'cess to 'im, an' we 've had
no coachman sence at all, at all.   An' it 's
sorry I am " —

The lady's flow of eloquence was interrupted
at this point by the appearance of Mr. Todd
himself, who had been informed of the men's
arrival.   He asked some questions in regard
to Wellington's qualifications and former experience, and in view of his recent arrival in
the city was willing to accept Mr. Peterson's
recommendation instead of a reference.   He
said a few words about the nature of the
work, and stated his willingness to pay Wellington the wages formerly allowed Mr. Peterson, thirty dollars a month and board and
lodging.

This handsome offer was eagerly accepted,
and it was agreed that Wellington's term of

service should begin immediately. Mr. Peterson, being familiar with the work, and financially interested, conducted the new coachman through the stables and showed him what he would have to do. The silver-mounted harness, the variety of carriages, the names of which he learned for the first time, the arrangements for feeding and watering the horses, — these appointments of a rich man's stable impressed Wellington very much, and he wondered that so much luxury should be wasted on mere horses. The room assigned to him, in the second story of the barn, was a finer apartment than he had ever slept in; and the salary attached to the situation was greater than the combined monthly earnings of himself and aunt Milly in their Southern home. Surely, he thought, his lines had fallen in pleasant places.

Under the stimulus of new surroundings Wellington applied himself diligently to work, and, with the occasional advice of Mr. Peterson, soon mastered the details of his employment. He found the female servants, with whom he took his meals, very amiable ladies. The cook, Mrs. Katie Flannigan, was a widow. Her husband, a sailor, had been lost at sea.

She was a woman of many words, and when she was not lamenting the late Flannigan's loss, — according to her story he had been a model of all the virtues, — she would turn the batteries of her tongue against the former coachman. This gentleman, as Wellington gathered from frequent remarks dropped by Mrs. Flannigan, had paid her attentions clearly susceptible of a serious construction. These attentions had not borne their legitimate fruit, and she was still a widow unconsoled, — hence Mrs. Flannigan's tears. The housemaid was a plump, good-natured German girl, with a pronounced German accent. The presence on washdays of a Bohemian laundress, of recent importation, added another to the variety of ways in which the English tongue was mutilated in Mr. Todd's kitchen. Association with the white women drew out all the native gallantry of the mulatto, and Wellington developed quite a helpful turn. His politeness, his willingness to lend a hand in kitchen or laundry, and the fact that he was the only male servant on the place, combined to make him a prime favorite in the servants' quarters.

It was the general opinion among Wellington's acquaintances that he was a single man.

He had come to the city alone, had never
been heard to speak of a wife, and to personal
questions bearing upon the subject of matrimony had always returned evasive answers.
Though he had never questioned the correct-
ness of the lawyer's opinion in regard to his
slave marriage, his conscience had never been
entirely at ease since his departure from the
South, and any positive denial of his married
condition would have stuck in his throat.
The inference naturally drawn from his reticence in regard to the past, coupled with his
expressed intention of settling permanently
in Groveland, was that he belonged in the
ranks of the unmarried, and was therefore
legitimate game for any widow or old maid
who could bring him down. As such game
is bagged easiest at short range, he received
numerous invitations to tea-parties, where he
feasted on unlimited chicken and pound cake.
He used to compare these viands with the
plain fare often served by aunt Milly, and
the result of the comparison was another item
to the credit of the North upon his mental
ledger. Several of the colored ladies who
smiled upon him were blessed with good looks,
and uncle Wellington, naturally of a suscep-

tible temperament, as people of lively imagination are apt to be, would probably have
fallen a victim to the charms of some woman of his own race, had it not been for a
strong counter-attraction in the person of
Mrs. Flannigan. The attentions of the lately
discharged coachman had lighted anew the
smouldering fires of her widowed heart, and
awakened longings which still remained unsatisfied. She was thirty-five years old, and
felt the need of some one else to love. She
was not a woman of lofty ideals; with her a
man was a man —

> "For a' that an' a' that;"

and, aside from the accident of color, uncle
Wellington was as personable a man as any
of her acquaintance. Some people might
have objected to his complexion; but then,
Mrs. Flannigan argued, he was at least half
white; and, this being the case, there was no
good reason why he should be regarded as
black.

Uncle Wellington was not slow to perceive
Mrs. Flannigan's charms of person, and appreciated to the full the skill that prepared
the choice tidbits reserved for his plate at
dinner. The prospect of securing a white

wife had been one of the principal induce-
ments offered by a life at the North ; but
the awe of white people in which he had been
reared was still too strong to permit his taking any active steps toward the object of his
secret desire, had not the lady herself come
to his assistance with a little of the native
coquetry of her race.

" Ah, Misther Braboy," she said one evening
when they sat at the supper table alone, — it
was the second girl's afternoon off, and she
had not come home to supper, — " it must be
an awful lonesome life ye 've been afther
l'adin', as a single man, wid no one to cook
fer ye, or look afther ye."

" It are a kind er lonesome life, Mis' Flannigan, an' dat 's a fac'.   But sence I had de
privilege er eatin' yo' cookin' an' 'joyin' yo'
society, I ain' felt a bit lonesome."

" Yer flatthrin' me, Misther Braboy.   An'
even if ye mane it " —

" I means eve'y word of it, Mis' Flannigan."

" An' even if ye mane it, Misther Braboy,
the time is liable to come when things 'll be
different ; for service is uncertain, Misther Braboy.   An' then you 'll wish you had some nice,

clean woman, 'at knowed how to cook an' wash
an' iron, ter look afther ye, an' make yer life
comfortable."

Uncle Wellington sighed, and looked at
her languishingly.

" It 'u'd all be well ernuff, Mis' Flannigan,
ef I had n' met you; but I don' know whar
I 's ter fin' a colored lady w'at 'll begin ter
suit me after habbin' libbed in de same house
wid you."

" Colored lady, indade! Why, Misther Braboy, ye don't nade ter demane yerself by
marryin' a colored lady — not but they 're as
good as anybody else, so long as they behave
themselves.   There 's many a white woman
'u'd be glad ter git as fine a lookin' man as ye
are."

" Now *you 're* flattrin' *me,* Mis' Flannigan," said Wellington.   But he felt a sudden
and substantial increase in courage when she
had spoken, and it was with astonishing ease
that he found himself saying : —

" Dey ain' but one lady, Mis' Flannigan,
dat could injuce me ter want ter change de
lonesomeness er my singleness fer de 'sponsi-
bilities er matermony, an' I 'm feared she 'd
say no ef I 'd ax her."

"Ye 'd better ax her, Misther Braboy, an' not be wastin' time a-wond'rin'. Do I know the lady?"

"You knows 'er better 'n anybody else, Mis' Flannigan. *You* is de only lady I 'd be satisfied ter marry after knowin' you. Ef you casts me off I 'll spen' de rest er my days in lonesomeness an' mis'ry."

Mrs. Flannigan affected much surprise and embarrassment at this bold declaration.

"Oh, Misther Braboy," she said, covering him with a coy glance, "an' it 's rale 'shamed I am to hev b'en talkin' ter ye ez I hev. It looks as though I 'd b'en doin' the coortin'. I did n't drame that I 'd b'en able ter draw yer affections to mesilf."

"I 's loved you ever sence I fell in yo' lap on de street car de fus' day I wuz in Groveland," he said, as he moved his chair up closer to hers.

One evening in the following week they went out after supper to the residence of Rev. Cæsar Williams, pastor of the colored Baptist church, and, after the usual preliminaries, were pronounced man and wife.

III

According to all his preconceived notions, this marriage ought to have been the acme of uncle Wellington's felicity. But he soon found that it was not without its drawbacks. On the following morning Mr. Todd was informed of the marriage. He had no special objection to it, or interest in it, except that he was opposed on principle to having husband and wife in his employment at the same time. As a consequence, Mrs. Braboy, whose place could be more easily filled than that of her husband, received notice that her services would not be required after the end of the month. Her husband was re ained in his place as coachman.

Upon the loss of her situatioi Mrs. Braboy decided to exercise the married woman's prerogative of letting her husband support her. She rented the upper floor of a small house in an Irish neighborhood. The newly wedded pair furnished their rooms on the installment plan and began housekeeping.

There was one little circumstance, however, that interfered slightly with their enjoyment of that perfect freedom from care which ought

to characterize a honeymoon. The people
who owned the house and occupied the lower
floor had rented the upper part to Mrs.
Braboy in person, it never occurring to them
that her husband could be other than a white
man. When it became known that he was
colored, the landlord, Mr. Dennis O'Flaherty,
felt that he had been imposed upon, and, at
the end of the first month, served notice upon
his tenants to leave the premises. When
Mrs. Braboy, with characteristic impetuosity,
inquired the meaning of this proceeding, she
was informed by Mr. O'Flaherty that he did
not care to live in the same house "wid
naygurs." Mrs. Braboy resented the epithet
with more warmth than dignity, and for a
brief space of time the air was green with
choice specimens of brogue, the altercation
barely ceasing before it had reached the point
of blows.

It was quite clear that the Braboys could
not longer live comfortably in Mr. O'Flaherty's house, and they soon vacated the premises, first letting the rent get a couple of
weeks in arrears as a punishment to the too
fastidious landlord. They moved to a small
house on Hackman Street, a favorite locality
with colored people.

For a while, affairs ran smoothly in the new home. The colored people seemed, at first, well enough disposed toward Mrs. Braboy, and she made quite a large acquaintance among them. It was difficult, however, for Mrs. Braboy to divest herself of the conscious-ness that she was white, and therefore superior to her neighbors. Occasional words and acts by which she manifested this feeling were noticed and resented by her keen-eyed and sensitive colored neighbors. The result was a slight coolness between them. That her few white neighbors did not visit her, she naturally and no doubt correctly imputed to disapproval of her matrimonial relations.

Under these circumstances, Mrs. Braboy was left a good deal to her own company. Owing to lack of opportunity in early life, she was not a woman of many resources, either mental or moral. It is therefore not strange that, in order to relieve her loneliness, she should occasionally have recourse to a glass of beer, and, as the habit grew upon her, to still stronger stimulants. Uncle Welling-ton himself was no teetotaler, and did not interpose any objection so long as she kept her potations within reasonable limits, and

was apparently none the worse for them;
indeed, he sometimes joined her in a glass.
On one of these occasions he drank a little
too much, and, while driving the ladies of
Mr. Todd's family to the opera, ran against a
lamp-post and overturned the carriage, to the
serious discomposure of the ladies' nerves,
and at the cost of his situation.

A coachman discharged under such circumstances is not in the best position for
procuring employment at his calling, and
uncle Wellington, under the pressure of
need, was obliged to seek some other means
of livelihood. At the suggestion of his friend
Mr. Johnson, he bought a whitewash brush, a
peck of lime, a couple of pails, and a hand-
cart, and began work as a whitewasher. His
first efforts were very crude, and for a while
he lost a customer in every person he worked
for. He nevertheless managed to pick up a
living during the spring and summer months,
and to support his wife and himself in comparative comfort.

The approach of winter put an end to the
whitewashing season, and left uncle Wellington dependent for support upon occasional jobs
of unskilled labor. The income derived from

these was very uncertain, and Mrs. Braboy
was at length driven, by stress of circumstances, to the washtub, that last refuge of
honest, able-bodied poverty, in all countries
where the use of clothing is conventional.

The last state of uncle Wellington was now
worse than the first. Under the soft firm-
ness of aunt Milly's rule, he had not been
required to do a great deal of work, prompt
and cheerful obedience being chiefly what was
expected of him. But matters were very different here. He had not only to bring in the
coal and water, but to rub the clothes and
turn the wringer, and to humiliate himself
before the public by emptying the tubs and
hanging out the wash in full view of the
neighbors ; and he had to deliver the clothes
when laundered.

At times Wellington found himself wondering if his second marriage had been a wise
one. Other circumstances combined to change
in some degree his once rose-colored conception of life at the North. He had believed
that all men were equal in this favored locality, but he discovered more degrees of inequal-
ity than he had ever perceived at the South.
A colored man might be as good as a white

man in theory, but neither of them was of any
special consequence without money, or talent,
or position. Uncle Wellington found a great
many privileges open to him at the North, but
he had not been educated to the point where
he could appreciate them or take advantage
of them ; and the enjoyment of many of them
was expensive, and, for that reason alone, as
far beyond his reach as they had ever been.
When he once began to admit even the possibility of a mistake on his part, these considerations presented themselves to his mind
with increasing force. On occasions when
Mrs. Braboy would require of him some unusual physical exertion, or when too frequent applications to the bottle had loosened
her tongue, uncle Wellington's mind would
revert, with a remorseful twinge of conscience,
to the *dolce far niente* of his Southern home ;
a film would come over his eyes and brain,
and, instead of the red-faced Irishwoman opposite him, he could see the black but comely
disk of aunt Milly's countenance bending
over the washtub ; the elegant brogue of Mrs.
Braboy would deliquesce into the soft dialect
of North Carolina ; and he would only be
aroused from this blissful reverie by a wet

shirt or a handful of suds thrown into his face, with which gentle reminder his wife would recall his attention to the duties of the moment.

There came a time, one day in spring, when there was no longer any question about it : uncle Wellington was desperately homesick.

Liberty, equality, privileges, — all were but as dust in the balance when weighed against his longing for old scenes and faces. It was the natural reaction in the mind of a middle-aged man who had tried to force the current of a sluggish existence into a new and radically different channel. An active, industrious man, making the change in early life, while there was time to spare for the waste of adaptation, might have found in the new place more favorable conditions than in the old. In Wellington age and temperament combined to prevent the success of the experiment ; the spirit of enterprise and ambition into which he had been temporarily galvanized could no longer prevail against the inertia of old habits of life and thought.

One day when he had been sent to deliver clothes he performed his errand quickly, and

boarding a passing street car, paid one of his
very few five-cent pieces to ride down to the
office of the Hon. Mr. Brown, the colored
lawyer whom he had visited when he first
came to the city, and who was well known
to him by sight and reputation.

"Mr. Brown," he said, "I ain' gitt'n' 'long
very well wid my ole 'oman."

"What's the trouble?" asked the lawyer,
with business-like curtness, for he did not
scent much of a fee.

"Well, de main trouble is she doan treat
me right. An' den she gits drunk, an' wuss'n
dat, she lays vi'lent han's on me. I kyars de
marks er dat 'oman on my face now."

He showed the lawyer a long scratch on the
neck.

"Why don't you defend yourself?"

"You don' know Mis' Braboy, suh; you
don' know dat 'oman," he replied, with a
shake of the head. "Some er dese yer w'ite
women is monst'us strong in de wris'."

"Well, Mr. Braboy, it's what you might
have expected when you turned your back
on your own people and married a white
woman. You weren't content with being
a slave to the white folks once, but you must

try it again. Some people never know when
they 've got enough. I don't see that there 's
any help for you ; unless," he added sugges-
tively, " you had a good deal of money."

" 'Pears ter me I heared somebody say
sence I be'n up heah, dat it wuz 'gin de law
fer w'ite folks an' colored folks ter marry."

" That was once the law, though it has
always been a dead letter in Groveland. In
fact, it was the law when you got married,
and until I introduced a bill in the legislature
last fall to repeal it. But even that law
did n't hit cases like yours. It was unlawful
to make such a marriage, but it was a good
marriage when once made."

" I don' jes' git dat th'oo my head," said
Wellington, scratching that member as though
to make a hole for the idea to enter.

" It 's quite plain, Mr. Braboy. It 's unlawful to kill a man, but when he 's killed
he 's just as dead as though the law permitted
it. I 'm afraid you have n't much of a case,
but if you 'll go to work and get twenty-five
dollars together, I 'll see what I can do for
you. We may be able to pull a case through
on the ground of extreme cruelty. I might
even start the case if you brought in ten
dollars."

Wellington went away sorrowfully. The laws of Ohio were very little more satisfactory than those of North Carolina. And as for the ten dollars, — the lawyer might as well have told him to bring in the moon, or a deed for the Public Square. He felt very, very low as he hurried back home to supper, which he would have to go without if he were not on hand at the usual supper-time.

But just when his spirits were lowest, and his outlook for the future most hopeless, a measure of relief was at hand. He noticed, when he reached home, that Mrs. Braboy was a little preoccupied, and did not abuse him as vigorously as he expected after so long an absence. He also perceived the smell of strange tobacco in the house, of a better grade than he could afford to use. He thought perhaps some one had come in to see about the washing; but he was too glad of a respite from Mrs. Braboy's rhetoric to imperil it by indiscreet questions.

Next morning she gave him fifty cents.

"Braboy," she said, "ye've be'n helpin' me nicely wid the washin', an' I'm going ter give ye a holiday. Ye can take yer hook an' line an' go fishin' on the breakwater. I'll fix

ye a lunch, an' ye need n't come back till
night. An' there 's half a dollar ; ye can buy
yerself a pipe er terbacky. But be careful
an' don't waste it," she added, for fear she
was overdoing the thing.

Uncle Wellington was overjoyed at this
change of front on the part of Mrs. Braboy ;
if she would make it permanent he did not
see why they might not live together very
comfortably.

The day passed pleasantly down on the
breakwater. The weather was agreeable, and
the fish bit freely. Towards evening Wellington started home with a bunch of fish that
no angler need have been ashamed of. He
looked forward to a good warm supper ; for
even if something should have happened
during the day to alter his wife's mood for
the worse, any ordinary variation would be
more than balanced by the substantial addition of food to their larder. His mouth
watered at the thought of the finny beauties
sputtering in the frying-pan.

He noted, as he approached the house, that
there was no smoke coming from the chimney.
This only disturbed him in connection with
the matter of supper. When he entered the

gate he observed further that the window-shades had been taken down.

" 'Spec' de ole 'oman's been house-cleanin'," he said to himself. "I wonder she did n' make me stay an' he'p 'er."

He went round to the rear of the house and tried the kitchen door. It was locked. This was somewhat of a surprise, and disturbed still further his expectations in regard to supper. When he had found the key and opened the door, the gravity of his next discovery drove away for the time being all thoughts of eating.

The kitchen was empty. Stove, table, chairs, wash-tubs, pots and pans, had vanished as if into thin air.

"Fo' de Lawd's sake!" he murmured in open-mouthed astonishment.

He passed into the other room, — they had only two, — which had served as bedroom and sitting-room. It was as bare as the first, except that in the middle of the floor were piled uncle Wellington's clothes. It was not a large pile, and on the top of it lay a folded piece of yellow wrapping-paper.

Wellington stood for a moment as if petrified. Then he rubbed his eyes and looked around him.

" W'at do dis mean ? " he said. " Is I er-
dreamin', er does I see w'at I 'pears ter see ? "
He glanced down at the bunch of fish which
he still held. " Heah 's de fish ; heah 's de
house; heah I is ; but whar 's de ole 'oman,
an' whar 's de fu'niture ?   *I* can't figure out
w'at dis yer all means."

He picked up the piece of paper and unfolded it. It was written on one side. Here
was the obvious solution of the mystery, —
that is, it would have been obvious if he could
have read it ; but he could not, and so his
fancy continued to play upon the subject.
Perhaps the house had been robbed, or the
furniture taken back by the seller, for it had
not been entirely paid for.

Finally he went across the street and called
to a boy in a neighbor's yard.

" Does you read writin', Johnnie ? "

" Yes, sir, I 'm in the seventh grade."

" Read dis yer paper fuh me."

The youngster took the note, and with much
labor read the following : —

" MR. BRABOY :

" In lavin' ye so suddint I have ter say
that my first husban' has turned up unix-

PERHAPS THE HOUSE HAD BEEN ROBBED

pected, having been saved onbeknownst ter me from a wathry grave an' all the money wasted I spint fer masses fer ter rist his sole an' I wish I had it back I feel it my dooty ter go an' live wid 'im again. I take the furnacher because I bought it yer close is yors I leave them and wishin' yer the best of luck I remane oncet yer wife but now agin

" Mrs. Katie Flannigan.

" N. B. I 'm lavin town terday so it won't be no use lookin' fer me."

On inquiry uncle Wellington learned from the boy that shortly after his departure in the morning a white man had appeared on the scene, followed a little later by a moving-van, into which the furniture had been loaded and carried away. Mrs. Braboy, clad in her best clothes, had locked the door, and gone away with the strange white man.

The news was soon noised about the street. Wellington swapped his fish for supper and a bed at a neighbor's, and during the evening learned from several sources that the strange white man had been at his house the afternoon of the day before. His neighbors intimated that they thought Mrs. Braboy's

departure a good riddance of bad rubbish,
and Wellington did not dispute the proposition.

Thus ended the second chapter of Wellington's matrimonial experiences. His wife's
departure had been the one thing needful to
convince him, beyond a doubt, that he had
been a great fool. Remorse and homesick-
ness forced him to the further conclusion that
he had been knave as well as fool, and had
treated aunt Milly shamefully. He was not
altogether a bad old man, though very weak
and erring, and his better nature now gained
the ascendency. Of course his disappointment had a great deal to do with his remorse;
most people do not perceive the hideousness
of sin until they begin to reap its consequences. Instead of the beautiful Northern
life he had dreamed of, he found himself
stranded, penniless, in a strange land, among
people whose sympathy he had forfeited, with
no one to lean upon, and no refuge from the
storms of life. His outlook was very dark,
and there sprang up within him a wild longing to get back to North Carolina, — back
to the little whitewashed cabin, shaded with
china and mulberry trees; back to the wood-

pile and the garden; back to the old cronies with whom he had swapped lies and tobacco for so many years. He longed to kiss the rod of aunt Milly's domination. He had purchased his liberty at too great a price.

The next day he disappeared from Groveland. He had announced his departure only to Mr. Johnson, who sent his love to his relations in Patesville.

It would be painful to record in detail the return journey of uncle Wellington — Mr. Braboy no longer — to his native town; how many weary miles he walked; how many times he risked his life on railroad trucks and between freight cars; how he depended for sustenance on the grudging hand of back-door charity. Nor would it be profitable or delicate to mention any slight deviations from the path of rectitude, as judged by conventional standards, to which he may occasionally have been driven by a too insistent hunger; or to refer in the remotest degree to a compulsory sojourn of thirty days in a city where he had no references, and could show no visible means of support. True charity will let these purely personal matters remain locked in the bosom of him who suffered them.

IV

Just fifteen months after the date when uncle Wellington had left North Carolina, a weather-beaten figure entered the town of Patesville after nightfall, following the railroad track from the north. Few would have recognized in the hungry-looking old brown tramp, clad in dusty rags and limping along with bare feet, the trim-looking middle-aged mulatto who so few months before had taken the train from Patesville for the distant North; so, if he had but known it, there was no necessity for him to avoid the main streets and sneak around by unfrequented paths to reach the old place on the other side of the town. He encountered nobody that he knew, and soon the familiar shape of the little cabin rose before him. It stood distinctly outlined against the sky, and the light streaming from the half-opened shutters showed it to be occupied. As he drew nearer, every familiar detail of the place appealed to his memory and to his affections, and his heart went out to the old home and the old wife. As he came nearer still, the odor of fried chicken floated out upon the air and set his mouth to water-

ing, and awakened unspeakable longings in
his half-starved stomach.

At this moment, however, a fearful thought
struck him; suppose the old woman had taken
legal advice and married again during his absence? Turn about would have been only
fair play. He opened the gate softly, and with
his heart in his mouth approached the window
on tiptoe and looked in.

A cheerful fire was blazing on the hearth,
in front of which sat the familiar form of
aunt Milly — and another, at the sight of
whom uncle Wellington's heart sank within
him. He knew the other person very well;
he had sat there more than once before uncle
Wellington went away. It was the minister
of the church to which his wife belonged.
The preacher's former visits, however, had
signified nothing more than pastoral courtesy,
or appreciation of good eating. His presence
now was of serious portent; for Wellington
recalled, with acute alarm, that the elder's
wife had died only a few weeks before his
own departure for the North. What was the
occasion of his presence this evening? Was
it merely a pastoral call? or was he courting?
or had aunt Milly taken legal advice and married the elder?

Wellington remembered a crack in the wall, at the back of the house, through which he could see and hear, and quietly stationed himself there.

" Dat chicken smells mighty good, Sis' Milly," the elder was saying ; " I can't fer de life er me see why dat low-down husban' er yo'n could ever run away f'm a cook like you. It 's one er de beatenis' things I ever heared. How he could lib wid you an' not 'preciate you *I* can't understan', no indeed I can't."

Aunt Milly sighed. " De trouble wid Wellin'ton wuz," she replied, " dat he did n' know when he wuz well off. He wuz alluz wishin' fer change, er studyin' 'bout somethin' new."

" Ez fer me," responded the elder earnestly, " I likes things what has be'n prove' an' tried an' has stood de tes', an' I can't 'magine how anybody could spec' ter fin' a better housekeeper er cook dan you is, Sis' Milly. I 'm a gittin' mighty lonesome sence my wife died. De Good Book say it is not good fer man ter lib alone, en it 'pears ter me dat you an' me mought git erlong tergether monst'us well."

Wellington's heart stood still, while he

listened with strained attention. Aunt Milly sighed.

" I ain't denyin', elder, but what I 've be'n kinder lonesome myse'f fer quite a w'ile, an' I doan doubt dat w'at de Good Book say 'plies ter women as well as ter men."

" You kin be sho' it do," averred the elder, with professional authoritativeness; " yas 'm, you kin be cert'n sho'."

" But, of co'se," aunt Milly went on, " havin' los' my ole man de way I did, it has tuk me some time fer ter git my feelin's straighten' out like dey oughter be."

" I kin 'magine yo' feelin's Sis' Milly," chimed in the elder sympathetically, " w'en you come home dat night an' foun' yo' chist broke open, an' yo' money gone dat you had wukked an' slaved fuh f'm mawnin' 'tel night, year in an' year out, an' w'en you foun' dat no-'count nigger gone wid his clo's an' you lef' all alone in de worl' ter scuffle 'long by yo'self."

" Yas, elder," responded aunt Milly, " I wa'n't used right. An' den w'en I heared 'bout his goin' ter de lawyer ter fin' out 'bout a defoce, an' w'en I heared w'at de lawyer said 'bout my not bein' his wife 'less he

wanted me, it made me so mad, I made up
my min' dat ef he ever put his foot on my do'-
sill ag'in, I 'd shet de do' in his face an' tell
'im ter go back whar he come f'm."

To Wellington, on the outside, the cabin
had never seemed so comfortable, aunt Milly
never so desirable, chicken never so appetizing, as at this moment when they seemed
slipping away from his grasp forever.

" Yo' feelin's does you credit, Sis' Milly,"
said the elder, taking her hand, which for a
moment she did not withdraw.   " An' de way
fer you ter close yo' do' tightes' ag'inst 'im is
ter take me in his place.   He ain' got no
claim on you no mo'.   He tuk his ch'ice
'cordin' ter w'at de lawyer tol' 'im, an' 'ter-
mine' dat he wa'n't yo' husban'.   Ef he
wa'n't yo' husban', he had no right ter take
yo' money, an' ef he comes back here ag'in
you kin hab 'im tuck up an' sent ter de penitenchy fer stealin' it."

Uncle Wellington's knees, already weak
from fasting, trembled violently beneath him.
The worst that he had feared was now likely
to happen.   His only hope of safety lay in
flight, and yet the scene within so fascinated
him that he could not move a step.

" It 'u'd serve him right," exclaimed aunt Milly indignantly, " ef he wuz sent ter de penitenchy fer life! Dey ain't nuthin' too mean ter be done ter 'im. What did I ever do dat he should use me like he did? "

The recital of her wrongs had wrought upon aunt Milly's feelings so that her voice broke, and she wiped her eyes with her apron.

The elder looked serenely confident, and moved his chair nearer hers in order the better to play the rôle of comforter. Wellington, on the outside, félt so mean that the darkness of the night was scarcely sufficient to hide him; it would be no more than right if the earth were to open and swallow him up.

" An' yet aftuh all, elder," said Milly with a sob, " though 1 knows you is a better man, an' would treat me right, I wuz so use' ter dat ole nigger, an' libbed wid 'im so long, dat ef he 'd open dat do' dis minute an' walk in, I 'm feared I 'd be foolish ernuff an' weak ernuff to forgive 'im an' take 'im back ag'in."

With a bound, uncle Wellington was away from the crack in the wall. As he ran round the house he passed the wood-pile and snatched up an armful of pieces.   A moment later he threw open the door.

"Ole 'oman," he exclaimed, "here's dat wood you tol' me ter fetch in!   Why, elder," he said to the preacher, who had started from his seat with surprise, "w'at's yo' hurry? Won't you stay an' hab some supper wid us?"

THE BOUQUET

MARY MYROVER's friends were somewhat surprised when she began to teach a colored school. Miss Myrover's friends are mentioned here, because nowhere more than in a Southern town is public opinion a force which cannot be lightly contravened. Public opinion, however, did not oppose Miss Myrover's teaching colored children; in fact, all the colored public schools in town — and there were several — were taught by white teachers, and had been so taught since the State had undertaken to provide free public instruction for all children within its boundaries. Previous to that time, there had been a Freedman's Bureau school and a Presbyterian missionary school, but these had been withdrawn when the need for them became less pressing. The colored people of the town had been for some time agitating their right to teach their own schools, but as yet the claim had not been conceded.

The reason Miss Myrover's course created some surprise was not, therefore, the fact that a Southern white woman should teach a colored school; it lay in the fact that up to this time no woman of just her quality had taken up such work. Most of the teachers of colored schools were not of those who had constituted the aristocracy of the old régime; they might be said rather to represent the new order of things, in which labor was in time to become honorable, and men were, after a somewhat longer time, to depend, for their place in society, upon themselves rather than upon their ancestors. Mary Myrover belonged to one of the proudest of the old families. Her ancestors had been people of distinction in Virginia before a collateral branch of the main stock had settled in North Carolina. Before the war, they had been able to live up to their pedigree; but the war brought sad changes. Miss Myrover's father — the Colonel Myrover who led a gallant but desperate charge at Vicksburg — had fallen on the battlefield, and his tomb in the white cemetery was a shrine for the family. On the Confederate Memorial Day, no other grave was so profusely decorated with flowers, and, in the oration pronounced, the name of Colonel Myrover was always used to illustrate the highest type of patriotic devotion and self-sacrifice. Miss Myrover's brother, too, had fallen in the conflict; but his bones lay in some unknown trench, with those of a thousand others who had fallen on the same field. Ay, more, her lover, who had hoped to come home in the full tide of victory and claim his bride as a reward for gallantry, had shared the fate of her father and brother. When the war was over, the remnant of the family found itself involved in the common ruin, — more deeply involved, indeed, than some others; for Colonel Myrover had believed in the ultimate triumph of his cause, and had invested most of his wealth in Confederate bonds, which were now only so much waste paper.

There had been a little left. Mrs. Myrover was thrifty, and had laid by a few hundred dollars, which she kept in the house to meet unforeseen contingencies. There remained, too, their home, with an ample garden and a well-stocked orchard, besides a considerable tract of country land, partly cleared, but productive of very little revenue.

With their shrunken resources, Miss Myrover and her mother were able to hold up their heads without embarrassment for some years after the close of the war. But when things were adjusted to the changed conditions, and the stream of life began to flow more vigorously in the new channels, they saw themselves in danger of dropping behind, unless in some way they could add to their meagre income. Miss Myrover looked over the field of employment, never very wide for women in the South, and found it occupied. The only available position she could be supposed prepared to fill, and which she could take without distinct loss of caste, was that of a teacher, and there was no vacancy except in one of the colored schools. Even teaching was a doubtful experiment; it was not what she would have preferred, but it was the best that could be done.

"I don't like it, Mary," said her mother. "It's a long step from owning such people to teaching them. What do they need with education? It will only make them unfit for work."

"They're free now, mother, and perhaps they'll work better if they're taught some-

thing. Besides, it's only a business arrangement, and does n't involve any closer contact
than we have with our servants."

" Well, I should say not !" sniffed the old
lady. " Not one of them will ever dare to presume on your position to take any liberties
with us. *I* 'll see to that."

Miss Myrover began her work as a teacher
in the autumn, at the opening of the school
year. It was a novel experience at first.
Though there had always been negro servants
in the house, and though on the streets colored
people were more numerous than those of her
own race, and though she was so familiar
with their dialect that she might almost be
said to speak it, barring certain characteristic
grammatical inaccuracies, she had never been
brought in personal contact with so many of
them at once as when she confronted the fifty
or sixty faces — of colors ranging from a
white almost as clear as her own to the darkest livery of the sun — which were gathered
in the schoolroom on the morning when she
began her duties. Some of the inherited
prejudice of her caste, too, made itself felt,
though she tried to repress any outward sign
of it; and she could perceive that the chil-

dren were not altogether responsive ; they,
likewise, were not entirely free from antago-
nism. The work was unfamiliar to her. She
was not physically very strong, and at the close
of the first day went home with a splitting
headache. If she could have resigned then
and there without causing comment or annoyance to others, she would have felt it a privilege to do so. But a night's rest banished
her headache and improved her spirits, and
the next morning she went to her work with
renewed vigor, fortified by the experience of
the first day.

Miss Myrover's second day was more satisfactory. She had some natural talent for
organization, though hitherto unaware of it,
and in the course of the day she got her
classes formed and lessons under way. In a
week or two she began to classify her pupils
in her own mind, as bright or stupid, mis-
chievous or well behaved, lazy or industrious,
as the case might be, and to regulate her dis-
cipline accordingly. That she had come of
a long line of ancestors who had exercised
authority and mastership was perhaps not
without its effect upon her character, and
enabled her more readily to maintain good

order in the school. When she was fairly
broken in, she found the work rather to her
liking, and derived much pleasure from such
success as she achieved as a teacher.

It was natural that she should be more attracted to some of her pupils than to others.
Perhaps her favorite — or, rather, the one
she liked best, for she was too fair and just
for conscious favoritism — was Sophy Tucker.
Just the ground for the teacher's liking for
Sophy might not at first be apparent. The
girl was far from the whitest of Miss Myrover's pupils; in fact, she was one of the darker
ones. She was not the brightest in intellect,
though she always tried to learn her lessons.
She was not the best dressed, for her mother
was a poor widow, who went out washing and
scrubbing for a living. Perhaps the real tie
between them was Sophy's intense devotion
to the teacher. It had manifested itself
almost from the first day of the school, in the
rapt look of admiration Miss Myrover always
saw on the little black face turned toward
her. In it there was nothing of envy, nothing of regret; nothing but worship for the
beautiful white lady — she was not especially
handsome, but to Sophy her beauty was

almost divine — who had come to teach her.
If Miss Myrover dropped a book, Sophy was
the first to spring and pick it up; if she
wished a chair moved, Sophy seemed to an-
ticipate her wish; and so of all the number-
less little services that can be rendered in a
schoolroom.

Miss Myrover was fond of flowers, and
liked to have them about her. The children
soon learned of this taste of hers, and kept
the vases on her desk filled with blossoms
during their season. Sophy was perhaps the
most active in providing them. If she could
not get garden flowers, she would make ex-
cursions to the woods in the early morning,
and bring in great dew-laden bunches of bay,
or jasmine, or some other fragrant forest
flower which she knew the teacher loved.

" When I die, Sophy," Miss Myrover said
to the child one day, " I want to be covered
with roses. And when they bury me, I 'm
sure I shall rest better if my grave is banked
with flowers, and roses are planted at my
head and at my feet."

Miss Myrover was at first amused at Sophy's
devotion; but when she grew more accustomed to it, she found it rather to her liking.

It had a sort of flavor of the old régime, and she felt, when she bestowed her kindly notice upon her little black attendant, some of the feudal condescension of the mistress toward the slave. She was kind to Sophy, and permitted her to play the rôle she had assumed, which caused sometimes a little jealousy among the other girls. Once she gave Sophy a yellow ribbon which she took from her own hair. The child carried it home, and cherished it as a priceless treasure, to be worn only on the greatest occasions.

Sophy had a rival in her attachment to the teacher, but the rivalry was altogether friendly. Miss Myrover had a little dog, a white spaniel, answering to the name of Prince. Prince was a dog of high degree, and would have very little to do with the children of the school; he made an exception, however, in the case of Sophy, whose devotion for his mistress he seemed to comprehend. He was a clever dog, and could fetch and carry, sit up on his haunches, extend his paw to shake hands, and possessed several other canine accomplishments. He was very fond of his mistress, and always, unless shut up at home, accompanied her to school, where he spent most of

his time lying under the teacher's desk, or, in
cold weather, by the stove, except when he
would go out now and then and chase an
imaginary rabbit round the yard, presumably
for exercise.

At school Sophy and Prince vied with each
other in their attentions to Miss Myrover.
But when school was over, Prince went away
with her, and Sophy stayed behind; for Miss
Myrover was white and Sophy was black,
which they both understood perfectly well.
Miss Myrover taught the colored children,
but she could not be seen with them in public. If they occasionally met her on the street,
they did not expect her to speak to them,
unless she happened to be alone and no other
white person was in sight. If any of the
children felt slighted, she was not aware of it,
for she intended no slight; she had not been
brought up to speak to negroes on the street,
and she could not act differently from other
people. And though she was a woman of
sentiment and capable of deep feeling, her
training had been such that she hardly expected to find in those of darker hue than
herself the same susceptibility — varying in
degree, perhaps, but yet the same in kind —

that gave to her own life the alternations of feeling that made it most worth living.

Once Miss Myrover wished to carry home a parcel of books. She had the bundle in her hand when Sophy came up.

" Lemme tote yo' bundle fer yer, Miss Ma'y?" she asked eagerly. " I 'm gwine yo' way."

" Thank you, Sophy," was the reply. " I 'll be glad if you will."

Sophy followed the teacher at a respectful distance. When they reached Miss Myrover's home, Sophy carried the bundle to the doorstep, where Miss Myrover took it and thanked her.

Mrs. Myrover came out on the piazza as Sophy was moving away. She said, in the child's hearing, and perhaps with the intention that she should hear : " Mary, I wish you would n't let those little darkeys follow you to the house. I don't want them in the yard. I should think you 'd have enough of them all day."

" Very well, mother," replied her daughter. " I won't bring any more of them. The child was only doing me a favor."

Mrs. Myrover was an invalid, and oppo-

sition or irritation of any kind brought on
nervous paroxysms that made her miser-
able, and made life a burden to the rest of
the household, so that Mary seldom crossed
her whims. She did not bring Sophy to the
house again, nor did Sophy again offer her
services as porter.

One day in spring Sophy brought her
teacher a bouquet of yellow roses.

"Dey come off'n my own bush, Miss Ma'y,"
she said proudly, " an' I did n' let nobody
e'se pull 'em, but saved 'em all fer you, 'cause
I know you likes roses so much. I 'm gwine
bring 'em all ter you as long as dey las'."

" Thank you, Sophy," said the teacher;
" you are a very good girl."

For another year Mary Myrover taught the
colored school, and did excellent service. The
children made rapid progress under her tui-
tion, and learned to love her well; for they
saw and appreciated, as well as children could,
her fidelity to a trust that she might have
slighted, as some others did, without much
fear of criticism. Toward the end of her
second year she sickened, and after a brief
illness died.

Old Mrs. Myrover was inconsolable. She

ascribed her daughter's death to her labors as teacher of negro children. Just how the color of the pupils had produced the fatal effects she did not stop to explain. But she was too old, and had suffered too deeply from the war, in body and mind and estate, ever to reconcile herself to the changed order of things following the return of peace; and, with an unsound yet perfectly explainable logic, she visited some of her displeasure upon those who had profited most, though passively, by her losses.

" I always feared something would happen to Mary," she said. " It seemed unnatural for her to be wearing herself out teaching little negroes who ought to have been working for her. But the world has hardly been a fit place to live in since the war, and when I follow her, as I must before long, I shall not be sorry to go."

She gave strict orders that no colored people should be admitted to the house. Some of her friends heard of this, and remonstrated. They knew the teacher was loved by the pupils, and felt that sincere respect from the humble would be a worthy tribute to the proudest. But Mrs. Myrover was obdurate.

"They had my daughter when she was alive," she said, "and they've killed her. But she's mine now, and I won't have them come near her. I don't want one of them at the funeral or anywhere around."

For a month before Miss Myrover's death Sophy had been watching her rosebush — the one that bore the yellow roses — for the first buds of spring, and, when these appeared, had awaited impatiently their gradual unfolding. But not until her teacher's death had they become full-blown roses. When Miss Myrover died, Sophy determined to pluck the roses and lay them on her coffin. Perhaps, she thought, they might even put them in her hand or on her breast. For Sophy remembered Miss Myrover's thanks and praise when she had brought her the yellow roses the spring before.

On the morning of the day set for the funeral, Sophy washed her face until it shone, combed and brushed her hair with painful conscientiousness, put on her best frock, plucked her yellow roses, and, tying them with the treasured ribbon her teacher had given her, set out for Miss Myrover's home.

She went round to the side gate — the

house stood on a corner — and stole up the path to the kitchen. A colored woman, whom she did not know, came to the door.

" W'at yer want, chile? " she inquired.

" Kin I see Miss Ma'y? " asked Sophy timidly.

" I don't know, honey. Ole Miss Myrover say she don't want no cullud folks roun' de house endyoin' dis fun'al. I 'll look an' see if she 's roun' de front room, whar de co'pse is. You sed down heah an' keep still, an' ef she 's upstairs maybe I kin git yer in dere a minute. Ef I can't, I kin put yo' bokay 'mongs' de res', whar she won't know nuthin' erbout it."

A moment after she had gone, there was a step in the hall, and old Mrs. Myrover came into the kitchen.

" Dinah! " she said in a peevish tone; " Dinah! "

Receiving no answer, Mrs. Myrover peered around the kitchen, and caught sight of Sophy.

" What are you doing here? " she demanded.

" I — I 'm-m waitin' ter see de cook, ma'am," stammered Sophy.

"The cook is n't here now. I don't know where she is. Besides, my daughter is to be buried to-day, and I won't have any one visiting the servants until the funeral is over. Come back some other day, or see the cook at her own home in the evening."

She stood waiting for the child to go, and under the keen glance of her eyes Sophy, feeling as though she had been caught in some disgraceful act, hurried down the walk and out of the gate, with her bouquet in her hand.

"Dinah," said Mrs. Myrover, when the cook came back, "I don't want any strange people admitted here to-day. The house will be full of our friends, and we have no room for others."

"Yas 'm," said the cook. She understood perfectly what her mistress meant; and what the cook thought about her mistress was a matter of no consequence.

The funeral services were held at St. Paul's Episcopal Church, where the Myrovers had always worshiped. Quite a number of Miss Myrover's pupils went to the church to attend the services. The building was not a large one. There was a small gallery at the rear, to which

colored people were admitted, if they chose to
come, at ordinary services; and those who
wished to be present at the funeral supposed
that the usual custom would prevail. They
were therefore surprised, when they went to
the side entrance, by which colored people
gained access to the gallery stairs, to be met
by an usher who barred their passage.

" I 'm sorry," he said, " but I have had
orders to admit no one until the friends of
the family have all been seated. If you wish
to wait until the white people have all gone
in, and there 's any room left, you may be
able to get into the back part of the gallery.
Of course I can't tell yet whether there 'll be
any room or not."

Now the statement of the usher was a very
reasonable one; but, strange to say, none of
the colored people chose to remain except
Sophy. She still hoped to use her floral
offering for its destined end, in some way,
though she did not know just how. She
waited in the yard until the church was filled
with white people, and a number who could
not gain admittance were standing about the
doors. Then she went round to the side of
the church, and, depositing her bouquet care-

fully on an old mossy gravestone, climbed up
on the projecting sill of a window near the
chancel.   The window was of stained glass,
of somewhat ancient make.   The church was
old, had indeed been built in colonial times,
and the stained glass had been brought from
England.   The design of the window showed
Jesus blessing little children.   Time had dealt
gently with the window, but just at the feet
of the figure of Jesus a small triangular piece
of glass had been broken out.   To this aper-
ture Sophy applied her eyes, and through it
saw and heard what she could of the services
within.

Before the chancel, on trestles draped in
black, stood the sombre casket in which lay
all that was mortal of her dear teacher.   The
top of the casket was covered with flowers ;
and lying stretched out underneath it she saw
Miss Myrover's little white dog, Prince.   He
had followed the body to the church, and,
slipping in unnoticed among the mourners,
had taken his place, from which no one had
the heart to remove him.

The white-robed rector read the solemn
service for the dead, and then delivered a
brief address, in which he dwelt upon the

uncertainty of life, and, to the believer, the
certain blessedness of eternity. He spoke
of Miss Myrover's kindly spirit, and, as an
illustration of her love and self-sacrifice for
others, referred to her labors as a teacher of
the poor ignorant negroes who had been placed
in their midst by an all-wise Providence, and
whom it was their duty to guide and direct
in the station in which God had put them.
Then the organ pealed, a prayer was said,
and the long cortége moved from the church
to the cemetery, about half a mile away,
where the body was to be interred.

When the services were over, Sophy sprang
down from her perch, and, taking her flowers,
followed the procession. She did not walk
with the rest, but at a proper and respectful
distance from the last mourner. No one noticed the little black girl with the bunch of
yellow flowers, or thought of her as interested in the funeral.

The cortége reached the cemetery and filed
slowly through the gate; but Sophy stood
outside, looking at a small sign in white
letters on a black background : —

"*Notice*. This cemetery is for white people only. Others please keep out."

Sophy, thanks to Miss Myrover's painstaking instruction, could read this sign very distinctly. In fact, she had often read it before. For Sophy was a child who loved beauty, in a blind, groping sort of way, and had sometimes stood by the fence of the cemetery and looked through at the green mounds and shaded walks and blooming flowers within, and wished that she might walk among them. She knew, too, that the little sign on the gate, though so courteously worded, was no mere formality; for she had heard how a colored man, who had wandered into the cemetery on a hot night and fallen asleep on the flat top of a tomb, had been arrested as a vagrant and fined five dollars, which he had worked out on the streets, with a ball-and-chain attachment, at twenty-five cents a day. Since that time the cemetery gate had been locked at night.

So Sophy stayed outside, and looked through the fence. Her poor bouquet had begun to droop by this time, and the yellow ribbon had lost some of its freshness. Sophy could see the rector standing by the grave, the mourners gathered round; she could faintly distinguish the solemn words with

"FOR WHITE PEOPLE ONLY. OTHERS PLEASE KEEP OUT"

which ashes were committed to ashes, and
dust to dust. She heard the hollow thud of
the earth falling on the coffin ; and she leaned
against the iron fence, sobbing softly, until
the grave was filled and rounded off, and the
wreaths and other floral pieces were disposed
upon it. When the mourners began to move
toward the gate, Sophy walked slowly down
the street, in a direction opposite to that
taken by most of the people who came out.

When they had all gone away, and the
sexton had come out and locked the gate
behind him, Sophy crept back. Her roses
were faded now, and from some of them the
petals had fallen. She stood there irresolute,
loath to leave with her heart's desire unsatisfied, when, as her eyes sought again the
teacher's last resting-place, she saw lying beside the new-made grave what looked like
a small bundle of white wool. Sophy's eyes
lighted up with a sudden glow.

"Prince! Here, Prince!" she called.

The little dog rose, and trotted down to
the gate. Sophy pushed the poor bouquet
between the iron bars. "Take that ter Miss
Ma'y, Prince," she said, "that's a good
doggie."

The dog wagged his tail intelligently, took the bouquet carefully in his mouth, carried it to his mistress's grave, and laid it among the other flowers. The bunch of roses was so small that from where she stood Sophy could see only a dash of yellow against the white background of the mass of flowers.

When Prince had performed his mission he turned his eyes toward Sophy inquiringly, and when she gave him a nod of approval lay down and resumed his watch by the graveside. Sophy looked at him a moment with a feeling very much like envy, and then turned and moved slowly away.

THE WEB OF CIRCUMSTANCE

I

WITHIN a low clapboarded hut, with an open front, a forge was glowing. In front a blacksmith was shoeing a horse, a sleek, well-kept animal with the signs of good blood and breeding. A young mulatto stood by and handed the blacksmith such tools as he needed from time to time. A group of negroes were sitting around, some in the shadow of the shop, one in the full glare of the sunlight. A gentleman was seated in a buggy a few yards away, in the shade of a spreading elm. The horse had loosened a shoe, and Colonel Thornton, who was a lover of fine horseflesh, and careful of it, had stopped at Ben Davis's blacksmith shop, as soon as he discovered the loose shoe, to have it fastened on.

"All right, Kunnel," the blacksmith called out. "Tom," he said, addressing the young man, "he'p me hitch up."

Colonel Thornton alighted from the buggy, looked at the shoe, signified his approval of the job, and stood looking on while the blacksmith and his assistant harnessed the horse to the buggy.

"Dat's a mighty fine whip yer got dere, Kunnel," said Ben, while the young man was tightening the straps of the harness on the opposite side of the horse. "I wush I had one like it. Where kin yer git dem whips?"

"My brother brought me this from New York," said the Colonel. "You can't buy them down here."

The whip in question was a handsome one. The handle was wrapped with interlacing threads of variegated colors, forming an elaborate pattern, the lash being dark green. An octagonal ornament of glass was set in the end of the handle. "It cert'n'y is fine," said Ben; "I wish I had one like it." He looked at the whip longingly as Colonel Thornton drove away.

"'Pears ter me Ben gittin' mighty blooded," said one of the bystanders, "drivin' a hoss an' buggy, an' wantin' a whip like Colonel Thornton's."

"What's de reason I can't hab a hoss an'

buggy an' a whip like Kunnel Tho'nton's, ef
I pay fer 'em?" asked Ben. "We colored
folks never had no chance ter git nothin'
befo' de wah, but ef eve'y nigger in dis town
had a tuck keer er his money sence de wah,
like I has, an' bought as much lan' as I has, de
niggers might 'a' got half de lan' by dis time,"
he went on, giving a finishing blow to a horse-
shoe, and throwing it on the ground to cool.

Carried away by his own eloquence, he did
not notice the approach of two white men
who came up the street from behind him.

"An' ef you niggers," he continued, raking
the coals together over a fresh bar of iron,
"would stop wastin' yo' money on 'scursions
to put money in w'ite folks' pockets, an' stop
buildin' fine chu'ches, an' buil' houses fer
yo'se'ves, you 'd git along much faster."

"You 're talkin' sense, Ben," said one of
the white men. "Yo'r people will never be
respected till they 've got property."

The conversation took another turn. The
white men transacted their business and went
away. The whistle of a neighboring steam
sawmill blew a raucous blast for the hour of
noon, and the loafers shuffled away in different directions.

"You kin go ter dinner, Tom," said the blacksmith. "An' stop at de gate w'en yer go by my house, and tell Nancy I 'll be dere in 'bout twenty minutes. I got ter finish dis yer plough p'int fus'."

The young man walked away. One would have supposed, from the rapidity with which he walked, that he was very hungry. A quarter of an hour later the blacksmith dropped his hammer, pulled off his leather apron, shut the front door of the shop, and went home to dinner. He came into the house out of the fervent heat, and, throwing off his straw hat, wiped his brow vigorously with a red cotton handkerchief.

"Dem collards smells good," he said, sniffing the odor that came in through the kitchen door, as his good-looking yellow wife opened it to enter the room where he was. "I 've got a monst'us good appetite ter-day. I feels good, too. I paid Majah Ransom de intrus' on de mortgage dis mawnin' an' a hund'ed dollahs besides, an' I spec's ter hab de balance ready by de fust of nex' Jiniwary; an' den we won't owe nobody a cent. I tell yer dere ain' nothin' like propputy ter make a pusson feel like a man. But w'at 's de matter wid yer, Nancy? Is sump'n' skeered yer?"

The woman did seem excited and ill at ease. There was a heaving of the full bust, a quickened breathing, that betokened suppressed excitement.

"I — I — jes' seen a rattlesnake out in de gyahden," she stammered.

The blacksmith ran to the door. "Which way? Whar wuz he?" he cried.

He heard a rustling in the bushes at one side of the garden, and the sound of a breaking twig, and, seizing a hoe which stood by the door, he sprang toward the point from which the sound came.

"No, no," said the woman hurriedly, "it wuz over here," and she directed her husband's attention to the other side of the garden.

The blacksmith, with the uplifted hoe, its sharp blade gleaming in the sunlight, peered cautiously among the collards and tomato plants, listening all the while for the ominous rattle, but found nothing.

"I reckon he's got away," he said, as he set the hoe up again by the door. "Whar's de chillen?" he asked with some anxiety. "Is dey playin' in de woods?"

" No," answered his wife, " dey 've gone ter de spring."

The spring was on the opposite side of the garden from that on which the snake was said to have been seen, so the blacksmith sat down and fanned himself with a palm-leaf fan until the dinner was served.

" Yer ain't quite on time ter-day, Nancy," he said, glancing up at the clock on the mantel, after the edge of his appetite had been taken off. " Got ter make time ef yer wanter make money. Did n't Tom tell yer I 'd be heah in twenty minutes ? "

" No," she said; " I seen him goin' pas'; he did n' say nothin'."

" I dunno w'at 's de matter wid dat boy," mused the blacksmith over his apple dumpling. " He 's gittin' mighty keerless heah lately; mus' hab sump'n' on 'is min', — some gal, I reckon."

The children had come in while he was speaking, — a slender, shapely boy, yellow like his mother, a girl several years younger, dark like her father: both bright-looking children and neatly dressed.

" I seen cousin Tom down by de spring," said the little girl, as she lifted off the pail

of water that had been balanced on her head.
" He come out er de woods jest ez we wuz
fillin' our buckets."

" Yas," insisted the blacksmith, " he's got
some gal on his min'."

II

The case of the State of North Carolina *vs.*
Ben Davis was called. The accused was led
into court, and took his seat in the prisoner's
dock.

" Prisoner at the bar, stand up."

The prisoner, pale and anxious, stood up.
The clerk read the indictment, in which it was
charged that the defendant by force and arms
had entered the barn of one G. W. Thornton,
and feloniously taken therefrom one whip, of
the value of fifteen dollars.

" Are you guilty or not guilty ? " asked the
judge.

" Not guilty, yo' Honah ; not guilty, Jedge.
I never tuck de whip."

The State's attorney opened the case. He
was young and zealous. Recently elected to
the office, this was his first batch of cases, and
he was anxious to make as good a record as

possible.   He had no doubt of the prisoner's
guilt.   There had been a great deal of petty
thieving in the county, and several gentlemen
had suggested to him the necessity for greater
severity in punishing it.   The jury were all
white men.   The prosecuting attorney stated
the case.

"We expect to show, gentlemen of the
jury, the facts set out in the indictment, —
not altogether by direct proof, but by a chain
of circumstantial evidence which is stronger
even than the testimony of eyewitnesses.   Men
might lie, but circumstances cannot.   We expect to show that the defendant is a man of
dangerous character, a surly, impudent fellow;
a man whose views of property are prejudicial
to the welfare of society, and who has been
heard to assert that half the property which
is owned in this county has been stolen, and
that, if justice were done, the white people
ought to divide up the land with the negroes;
in other words, a negro nihilist, a communist,
a secret devotee of Tom Paine and Voltaire, a
pupil of the anarchist propaganda, which, if
not checked by the stern hand of the law, will
fasten its insidious fangs on our social system,
and drag it down to ruin."

"We object, may it please your Honor," said the defendant's attorney. "The prosecutor should defer his argument until the testimony is in."

"Confine yourself to the facts, Major," said the court mildly.

The prisoner sat with half-open mouth, overwhelmed by this flood of eloquence. He had never heard of Tom Paine or Voltaire. He had no conception of what a nihilist or an anarchist might be, and could not have told the difference between a propaganda and a potato.

"We expect to show, may it please the court, that the prisoner had been employed by Colonel Thornton to shoe a horse; that the horse was taken to the prisoner's blacksmith shop by a servant of Colonel Thornton's; that, this servant expressing a desire to go somewhere on an errand before the horse had been shod, the prisoner volunteered to return the horse to Colonel Thornton's stable; that he did so, and the following morning the whip in question was missing; that, from circumstances, suspicion naturally fell upon the prisoner, and a search was made of his shop, where the whip was found secreted; that the prisoner denied that the whip was there, but when confronted with the evidence of his crime, showed by his confusion that he was guilty beyond a peradventure."

The prisoner looked more anxious; so much eloquence could not but be effective with the jury.

The attorney for the defendant answered briefly, denying the defendant's guilt, dwelling upon his previous good character for honesty, and begging the jury not to prejudge the case, but to remember that the law is merciful, and that the benefit of the doubt should be given to the prisoner.

The prisoner glanced nervously at the jury. There was nothing in their faces to indicate the effect upon them of the opening statements. It seemed to the disinterested listeners as if the defendant's attorney had little confidence in his client's cause.

Colonel Thornton took the stand and testified to his ownership of the whip, the place where it was kept, its value, and the fact that it had disappeared. The whip was produced in court and identified by the witness. He also testified to the conversation at the black-

smith shop in the course of which the prisoner had expressed a desire to possess a similar whip. The cross-examination was brief,
and no attempt was made to shake the Colonel's testimony.

The next witness was the constable who had
gone with a warrant to search Ben's shop.
He testified to the circumstances under which
the whip was found.

"He wuz brazen as a mule at fust, an'
wanted ter git mad about it. But when we
begun ter turn over that pile er truck in the
cawner, he kinder begun ter trimble; when
the whip-handle stuck out, his eyes commenced
ter grow big, an' when we hauled the whip
out he turned pale ez ashes, an' begun to
swear he did n' take the whip an' did n' know
how it got thar."

"You may cross-examine," said the prosecuting attorney triumphantly.

The prisoner felt the weight of the testimony, and glanced furtively at the jury, and
then appealingly at his lawyer.

"You say that Ben denied that he had
stolen the whip," said the prisoner's attorney,
on cross-examination. "Did it not occur to
you that what you took for brazen impudence

might have been but the evidence of conscious innocence?"

The witness grinned incredulously, revealing thereby a few blackened fragments of teeth.

"I've tuck up more'n a hundred niggers fer stealin', Kurnel, an' I never seed one yit that did n' 'ny it ter the las'."

"Answer my question. Might not the witness's indignation have been a manifestation of conscious innocence? Yes or no?"

"Yes, it mought, an' the moon mought fall — but it don't."

Further cross-examination did not weaken the witness's testimony, which was very damaging, and every one in the court room felt instinctively that a strong defense would be required to break down the State's case.

"The State rests," said the prosecuting attorney, with a ring in his voice which spoke of certain victory.

There was a temporary lull in the proceedings, during which a bailiff passed a pitcher of water and a glass along the line of jurymen. The defense was then begun.

The law in its wisdom did not permit the defendant to testify in his own behalf. There were no witnesses to the facts, but several were called to testify to Ben's good character. The colored witnesses made him out possessed of all the virtues. One or two white men testified that they had never known anything against his reputation for honesty.

The defendant rested his case, and the State called its witnesses in rebuttal. They were entirely on the point of character. One testified that he had heard the prisoner say that, if the negroes had their rights, they would own at least half the property. Another testified that he had heard the defendant say that the negroes spent too much money on churches, and that they cared a good deal more for God than God had ever seemed to care for them.

Ben Davis listened to this testimony with half-open mouth and staring eyes. Now and then he would lean forward and speak perhaps a word, when his attorney would shake a warning finger at him, and he would fall back helplessly, as if abandoning himself to fate ; but for a moment only, when he would resume his puzzled look.

The arguments followed. The prosecuting attorney briefly summed up the evidence, and characterized it as almost a mathematical proof of the prisoner's guilt. He reserved his eloquence for the closing argument.

The defendant's attorney had a headache, and secretly believed his client guilty. His address sounded more like an appeal for mercy than a demand for justice. Then the State's attorney delivered the maiden argument of his office, the speech that made his reputation as an orator, and opened up to him a successful political career.

The judge's charge to the jury was a plain, simple statement of the law as applied to circumstantial evidence, and the mere statement of the law foreshadowed the verdict.

The eyes of the prisoner were glued to the jury-box, and he looked more and more like a hunted animal. In the rear of the crowd of blacks who filled the back part of the room, partly concealed by the projecting angle of the fireplace, stood Tom, the blacksmith's assistant. If the face is the mirror of the soul, then this man's soul, taken off its guard in this moment of excitement, was full of lust and envy and all evil passions.

The jury filed out of their box, and into the jury room behind the judge's stand.

There was a moment of relaxation in the court room. The lawyers fell into conversation across the table. The judge beckoned to Colonel Thornton, who stepped forward, and they conversed together a few moments. The prisoner was all eyes and ears in this moment of waiting, and from an involuntary gesture on the part of the judge he divined that they were speaking of him. It is a pity he could not hear what was said.

"How do you feel about the case, Colonel?" asked the judge.

"Let him off easy," replied Colonel Thornton. "He's the best blacksmith in the county."

The business of the court seemed to have halted by tacit consent, in anticipation of a quick verdict. The suspense did not last long. Scarcely ten minutes had elapsed when there was a rap on the door, the officer opened it, and the jury came out.

The prisoner, his soul in his eyes, sought their faces, but met no reassuring glance; they were all looking away from him.

"Gentlemen of the jury, have you agreed upon a verdict?"

"We have," responded the foreman. The

clerk of the court stepped forward and took the fateful slip from the foreman's hand.

The clerk read the verdict: "We, the jury impaneled and sworn to try the issues in this cause, do find the prisoner guilty as charged in the indictment."

There was a moment of breathless silence. Then a wild burst of grief from the prisoner's wife, to which his two children, not understanding it all, but vaguely conscious of some calamity, added their voices in two long, discordant wails, which would have been ludicrous had they not been heart-rending.

The face of the young man in the back of the room expressed relief and badly concealed satisfaction. The prisoner fell back upon the seat from which he had half risen in his anxiety, and his dark face assumed an ashen hue. What he thought could only be surmised. Perhaps, knowing his innocence, he had not believed conviction possible; perhaps, conscious of guilt, he dreaded the punishment, the extent of which was optional with the judge, within very wide limits. Only one other person present knew whether or not he was guilty, and that other had slunk furtively from the court room.

Some of the spectators wondered why there should be so much ado about convicting a negro of stealing a buggy-whip. They had forgotten their own interest of the moment before. They did not realize out of what trifles grow the tragedies of life.

It was four o'clock in the afternoon, the hour for adjournment, when the verdict was returned. The judge nodded to the bailiff.

" Oyez, oyez! this court is now adjourned until ten o'clock to-morrow morning," cried the bailiff in a singsong voice. The judge left the bench, the jury filed out of the box, and a buzz of conversation filled the court room.

" Brace up, Ben, brace up, my boy," said the defendant's lawyer, half apologetically. " I did what I could for you, but you can never tell what a jury will do. You won't be sentenced till to-morrow morning. In the meantime I 'll speak to the judge and try to get him to be easy with you. He may let you off with a light fine."

The negro pulled himself together, and by an effort listened.

" Thanky, Majah," was all he said. He seemed to be thinking of something far away.

He barely spoke to his wife when she frantically threw herself on him, and clung to his neck, as he passed through the side room on his way to jail. He kissed his children mechanically, and did not reply to the soothing remarks made by the jailer.

III

There was a good deal of excitement in town the next morning. Two white men stood by the post office talking.

" Did yer hear the news? "

" No, what wuz it? "

" Ben Davis tried ter break jail las' night."

" You don't say so! What a fool! He ain't be'n sentenced yit."

" Well, now," said the other, " I 've knowed Ben a long time, an' he wuz a right good nigger. I kinder found it hard ter b'lieve he did steal that whip. But what 's a man's feelin's ag'in' the proof? "

They spoke on awhile, using the past tense as if they were speaking of a dead man.

" Ef I know Jedge Hart, Ben 'll wish he had slep' las' night, 'stidder tryin' ter break out'n jail."

At ten o'clock the prisoner was brought into court. He walked with shambling gait, bent at the shoulders, hopelessly, with downcast eyes, and took his seat with several other prisoners who had been brought in for sentence. His wife, accompanied by the children, waited behind him, and a number of his friends were gathered in the court room.

The first prisoner sentenced was a young white man, convicted several days before of manslaughter. The deed was done in the heat of passion, under circumstances of great provocation, during a quarrel about a woman. The prisoner was admonished of the sanctity of human life, and sentenced to one year in the penitentiary.

The next case was that of a young clerk, eighteen or nineteen years of age, who had committed a forgery in order to procure the means to buy lottery tickets. He was well connected, and the case would not have been prosecuted if the judge had not refused to allow it to be nolled, and, once brought to trial, a conviction could not have been avoided.

" You are a young man," said the judge gravely, yet not unkindly, " and your life is

yet before you. I regret that you should
have been led into evil courses by the lust for
speculation, so dangerous in its tendencies, so
fruitful of crime and misery. I am led to believe that you are sincerely penitent, and that,
after such punishment as the law cannot re-
mit without bringing itself into contempt,
you will see the error of your ways and follow
the strict path of rectitude. Your fault has
entailed distress not only upon yourself, but
upon your relatives, people of good name and
good family, who suffer as keenly from your
disgrace as you yourself. Partly out of consideration for their feelings, and partly because I feel that, under the circumstances,
the law will be satisfied by the penalty I shall
inflict, I sentence you to imprisonment in
the county jail for six months, and a fine
of one hundred dollars and the costs of this
action."

"The jedge talks well, don't he?" whispered one spectator to another.

"Yes, and kinder likes ter hear hisse'f
talk," answered the other.

"Ben Davis, stand up," ordered the judge.

He might have said "Ben Davis, wake up,"
for the jailer had to touch the prisoner on the

shoulder to rouse him from his stupor. He stood up, and something of the hunted look came again into his eyes, which shifted under the stern glance of the judge.

" Ben Davis, you have been convicted of larceny, after a fair trial before twelve good men of this county. Under the testimony, there can be no doubt of your guilt. The case is an aggravated one. You are not an ignorant, shiftless fellow, but a man of more than ordinary intelligence among your people, and one who ought to know better. You have not even the poor excuse of having stolen to satisfy hunger or a physical appetite. Your conduct is wholly without excuse, and I can only regard your crime as the result of a tendency to offenses of this nature, a tendency which is only too common among your people; a tendency which is a menace to civilization, a menace to society itself, for society rests upon the sacred right of property. Your opinions, too, have been given a wrong turn; you have been heard to utter sentiments which, if disseminated among an ignorant people, would breed discontent, and give rise to strained relations between them and their best friends, their old masters, who understand their real nature and their real needs, and to whose justice and enlightened guidance they can safely trust. Have you anything to say why sentence should not be passed upon you? "

" Nothin', suh, cep'n dat I did n' take de whip."

" The law, largely, I think, in view of the peculiar circumstances of your unfortunate race, has vested a large discretion in courts as to the extent of the punishment for offenses of this kind. Taking your case as a whole, I am convinced that it is one which, for the sake of the example, deserves a severe punishment. Nevertheless, I do not feel disposed to give you the full extent of the law, which would be twenty years in the penitentiary,[1] but, considering the fact that you have a family, and have heretofore borne a good reputation in the community, I will impose upon you the light sentence of imprisonment for five years in the penitentiary at hard labor. And I hope that this will be a warning to ycu and others who may be similarly

[1] There are no degrees of larceny in North Carolina, and the penalty for any offense lies in the discretion of the judge, to the limit of twenty years.

disposed, and that after your sentence has expired you may lead the life of a law-abiding citizen."

"O Ben! O my husband! O God!" moaned the poor wife, and tried to press forward to her husband's side.

"Keep back, Nancy, keep back," said the jailer. "You can see him in jail."

Several people were looking at Ben's face. There was one flash of despair, and then nothing but a stony blank, behind which he masked his real feelings, whatever they were.

Human character is a compound of tendencies inherited and habits acquired. In the anxiety, the fear of disgrace, spoke the nineteenth century civilization with which Ben Davis had been more or less closely in touch during twenty years of slavery and fifteen years of freedom. In the stolidity with which he received this sentence for a crime which he had not committed, spoke who knows what trait of inherited savagery? For stoicism is a savage virtue.

IV

One morning in June, five years later, a black man limped slowly along the old Lum-

berton plank road; a tall man, whose bowed
shoulders made him seem shorter than he was,
and a face from which it was difficult to guess
his years, for in it the wrinkles and flabbiness
of age were found side by side with firm white
teeth, and eyes not sunken, — eyes bloodshot,
and burning with something, either fever or
passion. Though he limped painfully with
one foot, the other hit the ground impatiently, like the good horse in a poorly
matched team. As he walked along, he was
talking to himself: —

"I wonder what dey 'll do w'en I git back?
I wonder how Nancy's s'ported the fambly
all dese years? Tuck in washin', I s'ppose, —
she was a monst'us good washer an' ironer.
I wonder ef de chillun 'll be too proud ter
reco'nize deir daddy come back f'um de pen-
etenchy? I 'spec' Billy must be a big boy
by dis time. He won' b'lieve his daddy ever
stole anything. I 'm gwine ter slip roun' an'
s'prise 'em."

Five minutes later a face peered cautiously
into the window of what had once been Ben
Davis's cabin, — at first an eager face, its
coarseness lit up with the fire of hope; a moment later a puzzled face; then an anxious,

fearful face as the man stepped away from
the window and rapped at the door.

" Is Mis' Davis home? " he asked of the
woman who opened the door.

" Mis' Davis don' live here. You er mistook in de house."

" Whose house is dis? "

" It b'longs ter my husban', Mr. Smith, —
Primus Smith."

" 'Scuse me, but I knowed de house some
years ago w'en I wuz here oncet on a visit,
an' it b'longed ter a man name' Ben Davis."

" Ben Davis — Ben Davis? — oh yes, I
'member now. Dat wuz de gen'man w'at
wuz sent ter de penitenchy fer sump'n er
nuther, — sheep-stealin', I b'lieve. Primus,"
she called, " w'at wuz Ben Davis, w'at useter
own dis yer house, sent ter de penitenchy
fer? "

" Hoss-stealin'," came back the reply in
sleepy accents, from the man seated by the
fireplace.

The traveler went on to the next house.
A neat-looking yellow woman came to the
door when he rattled the gate, and stood
looking suspiciously at him.

" W'at you want? " she asked.

" Please, ma'am, will you tell me whether a man name' Ben Davis useter live in dis neighborhood? "

" Useter live in de nex' house ; wuz sent ter de penitenchy fer killin' a man."

" Kin yer tell me w'at went wid Mis' Davis ? "

" Umph ! I 's a 'spectable 'oman, I is, en don' mix wid dem kind er people. She wuz 'n' no better 'n her husban'. She tuk up wid a man dat useter wuk fer Ben, an' dey 're livin' down by de ole wagon-ya'd, where no 'spectable 'oman ever puts her foot."

" An' de chillen ? "

" De gal 's dead. Wuz 'n' no better 'n she oughter be'n. She fell in de crick an' got drown' ; some folks say she wuz 'n' sober w'en it happen'. De boy tuck atter his pappy. He wuz 'rested las' week fer shootin' a w'ite man, an' wuz lynch' de same night. Dey wa'n't none of 'em no 'count after deir pappy went ter de penitenchy."

" What went wid de proputty ? "

" Hit wuz sol' fer de mortgage, er de taxes, er de lawyer, er sump'n, — I don' know w'at. A w'ite man got it."

The man with the bundle went on until he

came to a creek that crossed the road. He descended the sloping bank, and, sitting on a stone in the shade of a water-oak, took off his coarse brogans, unwound the rags that served him in lieu of stockings, and laved in the cool water the feet that were chafed with many a weary mile of travel.

After five years of unrequited toil, and unspeakable hardship in convict camps, — five years of slaving by the side of human brutes, and of nightly herding with them in vermin-haunted huts, — Ben Davis had become like them. For a while he had received occasional letters from home, but in the shifting life of the convict camp they had long since ceased to reach him, if indeed they had been written. For a year or two, the consciousness of his innocence had helped to make him resist the debasing influences that surrounded him. The hope of shortening his sentence by good behavior, too, had worked a similar end. But the transfer from one contractor to another, each interested in keeping as long as possible a good worker, had speedily dissipated any such hope. When hope took flight, its place was not long vacant. Despair followed, and black hatred of all mankind, hatred especially of the man to whom he attributed all his misfortunes. One who is suffering unjustly is not apt to indulge in fine abstractions, nor to balance probabilities. By long brooding over his wrongs, his mind became, if not unsettled, at least warped, and he imagined that Colonel Thornton had deliberately set a trap into which he had fallen. The Colonel, he convinced himself, had disapproved of his prosperity, and had schemed to destroy it. He reasoned himself into the belief that he represented in his person the accumulated wrongs of a whole race, and Colonel Thornton the race who had oppressed them. A burning desire for revenge sprang up in him, and he nursed it until his sentence expired and he was set at liberty. What he had learned since reaching home had changed his desire into a deadly purpose.

When he had again bandaged his feet and slipped them into his shoes, he looked around him, and selected a stout sapling from among the undergrowth that covered the bank of the stream. Taking from his pocket a huge clasp-knife, he cut off the length of an ordinary walking stick and trimmed it. The result

was an ugly-looking bludgeon, a dangerous
weapon when in the grasp of a strong man.

With the stick in his hand, he went on
down the road until he approached a large
white house standing some distance back from
the street. The grounds were filled with a
profusion of shrubbery. The negro entered
the gate and secreted himself in the bushes,
at a point where he could hear any one that
might approach.

It was near midday, and he had not eaten.
He had walked all night, and had not slept.
The hope of meeting his loved ones had been
meat and drink and rest for him. But as he
sat waiting, outraged nature asserted itself,
and he fell asleep, with his head on the rising
root of a tree, and his face upturned.

And as he slept, he dreamed of his child-
hood; of an old black mammy taking care of
him in the daytime, and of a younger face,
with soft eyes, which bent over him sometimes at night, and a pair of arms which
clasped him closely. He dreamed of his past,
— of his young wife, of his bright children.
Somehow his dreams all ran to pleasant
themes for a while.

Then they changed again. He dreamed

that he was in the convict camp, and, by an
easy transition, that he was in hell, consumed
with hunger, burning with thirst. Suddenly
the grinning devil who stood over him with
a barbed whip faded away, and a little white
angel came and handed him a drink of water.
As he raised it to his lips the glass slipped,
and he struggled back to consciousness.

"Poo' man! Poo' man sick, an' sleepy.
Dolly b'ing f'owers to cover poo' man up.
Poo' man mus' be hungry. W'en Dolly get
him covered up, she go b'ing poo' man some
cake."

A sweet little child, as beautiful as a cherub
escaped from Paradise, was standing over him.
At first he scarcely comprehended the words
the baby babbled out. But as they became
clear to him, a novel feeling crept slowly over
his heart. It had been so long since he had
heard anything but curses and stern words of
command, or the ribald songs of obscene mer-
riment, that the clear tones of this voice
from heaven cooled his calloused heart as the
water of the brook had soothed his blistered
feet. It was so strange, so unwonted a thing,
that he lay there with half-closed eyes while
the child brought leaves and flowers and laid

them on his face and on his breast, and arranged them with little caressing taps.

She moved away, and plucked a flower. And then she spied another farther on, and then another, and, as she gathered them, kept increasing the distance between herself and the man lying there, until she was several rods away.

Ben Davis watched her through eyes over which had come an unfamiliar softness. Under the lingering spell of his dream, her golden hair, which fell in rippling curls, seemed like a halo of purity and innocence and peace, irradiating the atmosphere around her. It is true the thought occurred to Ben, vaguely, that through harm to her he might inflict the greatest punishment upon her father; but the idea came like a dark shape that faded away and vanished into nothingness as soon as it came within the nimbus that surrounded the child's person.

The child was moving on to pluck still another flower, when there came a sound of hoof-beats, and Ben was aware that a horseman, visible through the shrubbery, was coming along the curved path that led from the gate to the house. It must be the man he was waiting for, and now was the time to wreak his vengeance. He sprang to his feet, grasped his club, and stood for a moment irresolute. But either the instinct of the convict, beaten, driven, and debased, or the influence of the child, which was still strong upon him, impelled him, after the first momentary pause, to flee as though seeking safety.

His flight led him toward the little girl, whom he must pass in order to make his escape, and as Colonel Thornton turned the corner of the path he saw a desperate-looking negro, clad in filthy rags, and carrying in his hand a murderous bludgeon, running toward the child, who, startled by the sound of footsteps, had turned and was looking toward the approaching man with wondering eyes. A sickening fear came over the father's heart, and drawing the ever-ready revolver, which according to the Southern custom he carried always upon his person, he fired with unerring aim. Ben Davis ran a few yards farther, faltered, threw out his hands, and fell dead at the child's feet.

Some time, we are told, when the cycle of years has rolled around, there is to be another golden age, when all men will dwell together in love and harmony, and when peace and righteousness shall prevail for a thousand years. God speed the day, and let not the shining thread of hope become so enmeshed in the web of circumstance that we lose sight of it ; but give us here and there, and now and then, some little foretaste of this golden age, that we may the more patiently and hopefully await its coming !

SELECTED ANN ARBOR PAPERBACKS

works of enduring merit

For a complete list of Ann Arbor Paperback titles write:

THE UNIVERSITY OF MICHIGAN PRESS / ANN ARBOR